INFURIATED

JR THOMPSON

FOREWORD

I realize many people believe the Irish slave trade was only a myth or that all Irish slaves were merely indentured servants. For that reason, I did extensive research on this subject prior to beginning my work on this historical fiction series.

I wrote *Brutalized* and *Infuriated* after reading *The Irish Slaves* by Rhetta Akamatsu, *Bound With An Iron Chain* by Anthony Vaver, *White Gold* by Giles Milton, and *They Were White and They Were Slaves* by Michael A. Hoffman II. I also received inspiration from many online sources.

Brutalized and *Infuriated* are based on historical events, but the characters and specific incidents come straight from my imagination.

I intentionally combined modern-day language with some of the terminology which would have been used during the colonial period in order to make these books easier to read.

CONTENTS

Cover designed by Lynn Andreozzi.

ISBN# 978-1-7337673-7-8

CHAPTER ONE

HORRIBLE BEGINNING

Excruciating pain knocked thirteen-year-old Callum McCarthy to his knees. His back arched as Master Levi Stone's flaming-hot branding iron seared the letters *S.L.* into his behind. The lad's flesh sizzled while emitting an aroma of burning hamburger meat. With a flurry of rapid, shallow breaths the young teenager bared his teeth while attempting to ignore the three light-skinned smoked Irish who busied themselves mocking his agony.

As soon as his new master released his arm, Callum fell on his face and grabbed his bottom. The freshly branded skin was so hot, the lad jerked his hand away. One of the slaves stooped down. In a slow, hushed, creepy voice, he said, "Now that your seat's nice and charred, it's learnin' time!"

Thinking at a normal pace with his skin ablaze was next to impossible. Callum sniffled while wiping snot off his upper lip. The pain was unlike anything he'd ever experienced. He shuddered as the slave's words replayed in his head. Whatever lesson awaited, the lad doubted he'd be permitted to put his clothes back on before it begun. How Master Levi Stone, or Uncle Keir if that's who the man really was, could think it okay to treat anyone this way was difficult to fathom.

"Ready, Duncan?" one of the other slaves asked. Duncan? That was the slow-speaking, broad-nosed, scar-faced, evil-eyed overseer's name? Callum would be sure to remember it for the rest of his days.

Speaking just as spookily as before, the man eagerly whispered, "You know I'm ready!" Still staring Callum in the eye, Duncan snickered every bit as slowly as he spoke while rising to his feet and sluggishly backing away.

Each of the other two slaves grabbed one of the lad's elbows. Still not taking his eyes off of Callum's for as long as a second, Duncan raised his volume, "On your feet, you filthy white nigger!"

Callum tried to comply, but fear fastened his knees to the ground. Within three seconds, the men were dragging Callum across the ground backward, with his knees skidding across the dirt and rocks as they went. The lad's knee pain paled in comparison to the mental anguish of not knowing where he was being taken or what else the light-skinned slaves might do to him.

Ten yards later, with his knees a bloody mess, Callum yelled, "I'll stand up!" The younger of the slaves paused to look at Duncan while the older one continued forward, creating a tug-of-war match between the two. "Let me go!" Callum demanded as the men tugged him in opposite directions. "I said I'll stand up!"

"Too late," Duncan argued. "Besides, you're just about to your destination. Cuddy, once you guys get him in place, tie him up good and tight. We don't need another one getting loose on us."

"I won't make that mistake again. Achan nearly killed me last time."

"And that was just a warning," Achan growled. "Come on, Cuddy, help me secure him."

Secure? Callum knew what that meant! Outnumbered or not, the lad refused to submit to an undeserved whipping, especially while in the buff. As soon as Cuddy and Achan relaxed their grips to fool with the ropes, the thirteen-year-old pulled free and attempted an escape. Five steps later, Duncan shoved him from behind, causing him to face-plant. Before Callum had time to do as much as roll over, Duncan dropped a knee in the small of his back. "Stupid move, cracker."

Infuriated, Callum attempted to buck the light-skinned slave off of him. Duncan grabbed Callum's right arm and twisted it so far behind his back, the lad feared it would snap. Sobbing, he screamed, "Let go! You're breaking my arm!"

"That'll be the least of your problems if you try something like that again."

Callum twisted his free hand around and dug his fingernails into Duncan's thigh. The slave laughed while grabbing the lad's hand and bending his fingers so far backward his knuckles were on the verge of becoming dislocated. Unwilling to give up the fight, Callum kicked with both legs, repeatedly thumping his feet against Duncan's back.

Achan laughed as he headed toward Callum's legs. "Gotta love new crackers! Here, let me help you with him, Duncan." The older overseer sat on Callum's feet. "Settle down, lad," he said sternly. "I'm not going to stand idly by and watch you abuse a man who's merely doing his job."

Oh, how wicked Callum was to get in the way of a man who was *merely doing his job!* What an idiotic thing to say! Callum tried to kick, buck, pinch, to do anything to retaliate against the men who pinned him to the ground, but his efforts proved futile. The light-skinned slaves held the lad in place until he wore himself out.

Even then, the slaves weren't too hasty to make things easier on the lad. "I'm going to test you now," Duncan said. "We can't let you up until you prove you're going to cooperate. Do you promise not to run anymore if we release you?"

"Yes!" Callum blubbered. "I won't go anywhere. I promise. Just let go of my arms. They're killing me!"

"And why should I believe you won't take off if we let you go?"

Callum lay in silence for a moment. Those men didn't know him. His word wouldn't mean anything to them. Raising his head, he made eye contact with Cuddy. Why was the man smiling? It didn't matter. Callum needed to come up with an answer. Something, anything that would convince the other two slaves to get off of him.

"I don't know if you'll believe anything I say, but the reason you caught up with me so quickly is because I can't hardly run. My knees are all tore up. My behind feels like it's on fire. The more I move, the more pain I feel."

"Hmm," Duncan replied. Speaking in a barely audible, yet creepy voice, he said, "I don't know. What do you think, Achan?"

For a moment, the air was filled with silence. Achan repositioned himself.

"There are three of you and only one of me," Callum said. "None of you are hurt; I am. You're all adults; I'm thirteen. I'm not going anywhere."

Achan raised up onto his knees. "I'm getting up, Duncan," he announced. "Cracker, if you fidget when I move, you'll be in far worse pain than you're in now. Got me?"

"Yes, sir," Callum said through gritted teeth. As much as the lad wanted to retaliate, he didn't move a muscle as Achan slowly got off him. He could only hope full compliance would work to his advantage.

Once Achan was on his feet, he said, "Good job, cracker. Since you stayed still, Duncan's gonna release your left arm and place it at your side. When he does, let that arm fall limp. Got me?"

"Yes, sir," Callum agreed. As soon as the lad's arm began to move, his shoulder popped. Even though the pain produced by that pop didn't bring insufferable pain, the lad's shoulder throbbed violently, his wrist hurt something fierce, and his fingers were going numb. Callum broke into a new fit of uncontrollable sobbing.

After three minutes of wailing without offering the slightest amount of physical resistance, Achan said, "Gentlemen, I believe we're making progress. Cracker, Duncan's about to release your other arm and then he's going to get off your back. Don't move until I tell you to. Got me?"

Callum nodded.

Slowly, Duncan moved the lad's right arm next to his side. Callum let out a painful sigh, but didn't move. Duncan shifted his weight, temporarily pushing his knee even further into the lad's back. Callum let out an agonizing groan, but kept his body still and refrained from mouthing off.

Moments later, Duncan placed one hand on each of Callum's while removing his knee from the lad's back. As he took his hands away, Achan said, "When I give the word, cracker, get on your hands and knees and crawl back to the big pine. Got me?"

"Yes, sir," Callum cried with a slight nod, hoping that direction didn't mean what he thought it did. Surely the men would cut him a break after everything he'd gone through, especially since he was now complying with their every direction.

"Now, lad!" Achan ordered.

Wasting no time, Callum hustled to his hands and knees. With every muscle in his body aching, his bottom feeling like someone was holding a torch to it, and his knees stinging from being dragged across the ground, Callum forced himself to crawl back to the tree he had fled from only moments before. How he hoped being forced to return there was nothing more than a scare tactic!

Stopping at its base, Callum twisted his head around to face the three light-skinned slaves as well as his new stone-faced master. "Stand up and face the tree," Achan commanded.

Trembling, Callum obeyed. If only he could figure out what he had done wrong! He hadn't given any dirty looks, spoken out of turn, or rebelled against his new master. As best he could tell, he hadn't done anything to offend anybody.

Seeing the thick rope dangling over a tree branch in front of him, Callum swallowed hard. Cuddy circled in front of him and grabbed his arms. Callum's instincts said it was time to either fight or take flight, but his body refused to do either. The lad allowed Cuddy to forcefully wrap a rope around his hands and wrists before tying it so tightly it cut off his circulation.

With chattering teeth, Callum looked over his shoulder.

"Alright, Duncan," Achan said. "It's time to teach that lesson. Stripe this filthy white nigger from shoulder to ankle." He paused and chuckled for a second. "Hope you're ready to make friends with the whip, cracker."

Callum furiously shook his head. "No! Please, no! Please, sirs! I'll do whatever you want!"

"You've got that right," Duncan chuckled evilly. Lowering his voice and slowing his speech, he added, "And right now, what I want is for you to put on a good show for me and my friends."

The young teenager couldn't turn his eyes back toward the pine. Instead, wide-eyed, he watched as Duncan, at the pace of an elderly praying mantis, took a few steps to his right and picked up a rather well-worn whip. "This is gonna be the highlight of my week," Duncan teased, strutting up behind the lad. Duncan touched the end of the whip to Callum's right shoulder and slowly slid it diagonally down the lad's back, stopping only when it reached his lower left hip. "This might be a good place to start," he laughed. "Unless I decide that area where you just got branded would make a better target. Wonder how many times I could hit the same spot?"

Callum's knees knocked together. Those three light-skinned slaves may have found his predicament amusing; he found it mortifying. In a fit of hysteria, the lad begged for mercy, but his panic-stricken sobs left his words impossible to make out.

"You'll toughen up," Duncan said in a loud whisper before taking several steps backward.

Callum knew what that meant. The beating was about to begin. Turning his head, he closed his eyes and bared his teeth.

Duncan cracked the whip, cutting Callum's flesh just above the new letters decorating his backside. A harrowing yelp escaped his lips. It was the first time a whip had ever hit him below the waistline, and wow, was that spot tender!

Achan clapped his hands together several times. "Yes!" he shouted. "That's how it's done! Hit that white nigger again!"

Callum squeezed his eyes as tight as he could get them. If that whip were to connect with his already burning bottom, he wouldn't be able to take it. Oh, how he hoped Duncan wasn't truly going to aim for it! That last lash was so close.

Cuddy hollered, "Hold on!" Even though he knew better, Callum hoped Cuddy would somehow stop the beating. Instead, the younger light-skinned overseer laughed wickedly, "Let me move over here in front of him. I want to see his face when he gets hit!"

The teenager opened his eyes, and relaxed his breathing for a moment as Cuddy repositioned himself. "You guys should see this," he laughed. "This cracker's got drool running down his chin. Unless it's snot from all that boo-hooing!"

Callum looked over his shoulder again. Achan remained in position and grew quiet as Duncan drew the whip back.

Taking advantage of the tiny amount of slack in the rope, the lad pulled his body tight against the tree. The move did nothing to soften the next blow. The whip connected with Callum's mid-back, wrapped around, and tore a chunk from his side. The lad squalled.

As Callum's eyes popped open, he found Cuddy raising two closed fists high in the air as if declaring some sort of victory.

Before the lad could ready himself, the whip tore into him a third time with much greater force than before. Buckets of tears streaked Callum's face. "Please, I'll do anything! Please, please! Don't do this to me!" he screamed, looking Duncan in the eye.

Duncan laughed creepily before softly and ever-so-slowly muttering, "We're just getting started, you filthy white nigger. All that screaming isn't going to help you one bit." He pulled the whip back and held it there for a moment. "This time I'm going for the leg!"

Callum's rapid, shallow breathing returned. "Don't! Please! Stop!" he screamed in horror. It was too late. Duncan already had the whip in the air. It tore into the tops of Callum's thighs. The lad jumped and wrapped both legs around the pine's trunk.

The three light-skinned slaves laughed as if Callum's behavior was the funniest thing they'd ever seen.

The cycle of laughter, lashing, and screaming continued for another fifteen minutes and would have gone much longer had Master Levi not stepped in. "That's enough, Duncan. I'm sure this cracker knows who's in charge now."

Stepping closer to Callum, he said, "Look at me, you piece of filthy white trash."

Callum looked in his direction, but the tears greatly distorted his vision.

"The name Callum isn't fitting for you. No, sir. That name belongs to somebody who's stout, hard-working, intelligent. You need a name that's better suited to a white nigger who's weak and cowardly, foolish, and void of any admirable qualities."

His name wasn't suitable? Nobody else had ever had a problem with it. Callum remembered the lad he met on his way to the last auction block. The one who bragged about refusing to acknowledge the new name his master had given him, no matter how many times that man beat him for it. That lad must have had a thick hide. Callum only wished he had the same amount of courage. But there was no time to think on such things.

"Now what should I call you? Hannibal? No. Sounds like someone more mature than you are. Cotton sounds soft and delicate. That might be a good match, but you're so stupid you'd probably take the name as a compliment."

Callum was more confused than ever. Up until that very moment, he struggled to believe Master Levi Stone really was who he claimed to be. He looked, sounded, and carried himself so much like Uncle Keir, it seemed impossible it wasn't him. If the man were the uncle he hadn't seen in years, he might not recognize the lad's face, but surely, he'd know the name. Perhaps Callum had been mistaken. Afterall, this man had a full beard, and he'd never seen Uncle Keir with one.

Master Levi continued, "Silas, now that's a nice name. Too nice for the likes of you. Finney? Yes. I believe that's it. You look like a Finney to me. Starting right now, that's your name."

With tears still streaming down his face and his upper lip quivering, Callum stared blankly at his uncle's look-alike.

"You will respond to your new name, cracker. If you don't, I'm sure Duncan here wouldn't mind giving you another lesson before Cuddy takes you down off this tree. Are you going to answer to Finney? What's it gonna be, cracker?"

CHAPTER TWO

MEETING THE BUNKMATES

Finney sounded like the name of a weed. The lad hated it. But not as much as he hated that whip, the cruel light-skinned smoked Irish, or Master Levi Stone.

Dragging himself through the doorway of what the Stone's referred to as the white nigger cabin, Finney gently tossed his shirt onto the filthiest table he'd ever seen before cautiously attempting to slide his breeches back on. What was normally an easy task now seemed all but impossible. Every time his breeches came in contact with another cut or bruise, the lad would let out a gasp, close his eyes, regain his composure, and try again. It didn't take long before he gave up on that idea altogether. Taking the breeches back off, he tossed them next to his shirt.

The white nigger cabin was full of beds. Not knowing which, if any, was his, Finney pushed a hat and a pair of dirty stockings off a chair by the table and took a seat. Wow, was that ever a mistake! As soon as his behind made contact with the chair, Finney hopped up. Between the burn and the freshly torn skin, sitting wasn't going to be possible for quite some time.

Carefully, the lad lowered himself down, moved a pair of mud-covered shoes, some tattered breeches, a shirt, and a pair of suspenders out of his path, and laid on his belly. Resting his chin on his hands, Finney bawled like a baby. It wasn't so much the pain as it was the thoughts of how cruel Master Levi Stone and the light-skinned smoked Irish had been. If that's how they treated a slave just for being new, he would hate to imagine how they might handle one whom they determined was in need of discipline. Finney dreaded the thoughts of spending as much as another day on such a horrible plantation.

Eventually, the lad cried himself to sleep. Sadly, about half an hour into his nap, he had a horrific nightmare. The branding iron was approaching his bare skin. The lad cringed. His entire body trembled as he remembered what that felt like, how it sounded, and the putrid smell it had brought. The ordeal was worse in his nightmare than it had been in real life. Finney caught a glimpse of the man who held him so tightly with one hand while preparing to brand him with the other. It was Uncle Keir, and he said, "Don't expect me to go lighter on you just because you're kin. If anything, I'll take less off of you than I will any of these other white niggers." Finney trembled from fear and shock. How was it even possible that Uncle Keir could live such a double life?

Just before the branding iron made contact, voices from somewhere just outside the cabin woke Callum from his nightmare. A large group of folks were coming his way. He couldn't make out what any of them were saying, but it sounded like they were in high spirits.

Finney hoped the crowd was going to bypass the white nigger cabin. The last thing he wanted was company. But something told him he was going to have guests whether he wanted them or not. The lad knew practically everyone on the plantation had already seen him fully unclothed but he didn't want them to see him that way a second time. Oh, how badly he wanted to get off of that floor and to put his clothes on! But he'd already tried that. There were only two choices. Stay laying on the floor, where half of his body was visible to all who entered, or stand up and put his entire body on display. Finney chose the former.

It wasn't long before the door opened, and twenty-five or thirty white slaves poured through it. One by one, they stopped talking upon seeing Finney. All but one woman, who walked over and said, "I'm sorry they did this to you." She paused as if trying to decide what to say next. The lady was taller than most of the men he had ever seen, she had broad shoulders and bulging biceps. Even so, there was a gentle spirit about her. "Can I clean your wounds for you?" she asked.

Humiliation would be the best word to describe Finney's feelings at that moment. Truthfully, he didn't want anyone touching his naked body — especially anyone of the female variety. But to say no to the first person on the plantation who had shown him any kindness seemed a foolish move.

Swallowing his pride, Finney said, "I would appreciate that, ma'am."

She giggled, "Please, child. Call me Cherish. That's the name everybody here knows me by."

Cherish was a far nicer name than Finney, the lad thought to himself as the kind lady walked away and spoke to a man he assumed was her husband, "Would you or one of the lads mind fetching a pail of water for me?"

"I'll get it," the fellow said. "Is the new lad going to be okay?"

"I'm sure he will be," Cherish replied. "He's lost a lot of blood, and you know Master Levi's rules. Finney won't be allowed to eat until he's been here a full twenty-four hours."

Finney hated when people talked about him as if he weren't right there in the same room with them. But speaking up was not something he felt comfortable doing.

"Should I try to find him some clothes, Momma?" A little boy who couldn't have been any older than six asked, walking over and staring nervously at Finney as he spoke.

"That's awfully kind of you, Henry. He's already been issued a set of clothes, but I don't think he's quite ready to wear anything just yet."

Up until hearing those conversations, Finney had no idea he would forego food for twenty-four hours. Nor had he given much thought to the fact he would have to go all night, and possibly the entire next day or two without any clothes on while sharing a cabin with a host of strangers.

Henry put his hands on his hips, "I hate Master Levi and his mulattos!"

"We're not supposed to hate anybody," Cherish scolded.

"They hate us! Why can't we hate 'em back?"

"Two wrongs never make a right, Henry. You know that!"

"But, Momma! They're always whippin' on us white niggers—"

Cherish cut him off, "Regardless of what Master Levi Stone, the mulattos, or even the smoked Irish call us, we *are not* white niggers. We are human beings, created in the image of the Almighty God. Don't you ever let me hear those kinds of words come out of your mouth again. Do you hear me?"

"Yes, ma'am," Henry said.

"And to set the record straight," Cherish continued, "none of the mulattos have ever taken a whip to you, so to say they're always whipping on *us* isn't exactly honest either."

Just then, the man who had volunteered to fetch the water returned with a pail in his hand. "Here you go," he said.

"Thank you, Newt," Cherish replied. "Would you mind setting it next to the lad for me?"

"My pleasure, sweetheart. I'll set it right here on this stack of cans."

Finney rolled his eyes and turned to face the wall, hoping to avoid further conversation. The less people got close to him, the happier he would be.

"Momma," Henry said, still not finished with his end of the talk. "Is it okay if I just wish Master Levi would take another trip? Maybe one that lasts even longer than his last one? And that maybe he takes the mulattos with him this time?"

Cherish giggled, "I suppose that would be okay. Sometimes I wish that myself. But we should probably shift our focus to the situation at hand."

Finney hoped Henry wouldn't drop it. He wasn't ready to have anybody tend his wounds. The more that little lad talked, the more time he would have to mentally prepare for what was coming next.

Henry plopped down next to him, knocking over somebody's beaker. "People need to stop leaving their stuff laying everywhere," he said, setting it back in place. "What's your name?"

"Call—," the lad caught himself. "It was Callum, but now it's Finney."

"Finney's a nice name. But I like Callum better."

As humiliated and sore as he was, Finney couldn't help but crack a smile. "Me too," he said.

"You gonna pay those mulattos back when you're bigger?"

"Maybe," Finney said. "To be honest though, I don't even know what a mulatto is."

"I'll answer that one for you, and after that I believe we've heard enough questions," Cherish interrupted. "A mulatto is someone who has one smoked Irish parent and one parent who's a cracker. On this plantation, Master Levi has chosen three men as his overseers. They're all mulattos. I'm sure you've noticed how they're too light colored to be called smoked Irish, but not light enough to be crackers?"

"Yes, ma'am," Finney said.

"Now that we have that settled, Henry, I told you to get ready for bed. Now scoot!"

"But, Momma!"

Cherish snapped her fingers, and Henry walked away.

Finney was thankful to have at least a moment of silence, even if that's all it was. "I can see you're in a lot of pain, Finney," Newt said. "I'm not going to lie to you. Those wounds are going to hurt for a long while. But my wife has a heart for doctoring people, and she'll help get the healing process started for you."

Even though the man was extraordinarily kind, Finney wanted to be left alone. He didn't speak a word.

That didn't stop Newt from continuing to ramble. "You took that beating better than some I've seen," he said. "You proved yourself a man out there."

Finney didn't feel like a man, no matter what Newt or anybody else thought. He had cried and screamed and tried everything he could to get out of that lashing. If he had done better than others, he would hate to have seen how they handled it.

Cherish walked back over and joined them. "This water's going to be cold, Finney," she said. "But cold water is better than none at all. Newt, would you mind extending a hand for Finney to grab hold of?"

"Sure. Here you go, Finney," the man said.

With his face to the wall, Finney didn't see the man's hand reaching toward him.

"Listen, child," Cherish said. "When I clean these wounds, that pain you're feeling right now is going to get much worse. I don't want you screaming; I'd rather you squeeze Newt's arm."

"I can handle it," Finney said. "I won't scream, and I don't need to hold onto anybody."

"Okay," Cherish said gently. "I'm going to start with this gash on your right shoulder. Are you ready?"

"Yes, ma'am," Finney replied.

"I told you to call me Cherish," the lady insisted. "We used to address the mistress as ma'am. And that woman is nobody I want to get confused with."

Finney hissed and panted even though Cherish barely dabbed his cut with a wet cloth. Turning to face Newt, he reached toward the man.

"I thought you might change your mind," Newt said, extending his hand to the lad once more.

Finney squeezed as hard as he could while squinting his eyes and gritting his teeth. Tensing his entire body, he said, "I'm ready. Let's do this."

Just as the rag brushed his cut a second time, Henry knelt down and patted his arm, "Everything's going to be okay," he said. "You're tough."

"Didn't I tell you to get ready for bed?" Cherish scolded.

"Yes, Momma. And I am ready."

"Why aren't you in bed yet then?"

"You didn't tell me to get in bed. Just to get ready for it. Can Finney tell me a bedtime story?"

Finney chuckled. What was with this kid?

"Not tonight," Cherish said. "Go to bed, and go to sleep. Do I make myself clear?"

"Yes, Momma."

CHAPTER THREE

CONTAGIOUS OPTIMISM

The agony intensified with each passing hour. Cherish wiped all the excess blood off, but that did nothing to ease Finney's pain. The part of the lad's bottom where Master Levi Stone had burned his initials felt as though it was on fire. The lad's back and legs throbbed continuously due to the thrashing they had received, his hands and wrists hurt from where he had pulled and tugged trying to free himself during the whipping, and his stomach ached due to a lack of nourishment.

The anguish penetrated much further than the flesh. Stripped of both his clothes and dignity, Finney felt sub-human. He had considered Master Cyrus a wicked-hearted control freak, but now, after how he had been treated by the mulattos and the planter, the Gillcrests didn't seem half as bad as he had thought.

Back in Dublin, the lad's peers teased him about his dirty hair and thick eyebrows on a daily basis. Upon arrival to the Gillcrest's plantation, Master Cyrus took an immediate liking to the idea of physically abusing the lad. And now that he'd moved to another plantation, things were even worse. Perhaps Master Stone and the mulattos weren't the horrible people Finney made them out to be. Maybe he deserved the harsh treatment for being too ugly and poor, the son of a drunkard, and for being from Ireland. Perhaps it was his red-tinted hair, pale skin, and blue eyes.

Every time the lad thought he had run out of tears, another one fell on his cheek. In too much pain to wipe them away, he allowed the droplets to coat his face throughout most of the night. But the last tear that fell was different. Unlike the others, it didn't go unnoticed.

Someone knelt on the floor next to him. With the rest of the shack silent, save those who were lightly snoring, a young man near Finney's age whispered, "I can't take the pain away, but is there anything I can do to make you feel better?"

Finney shrugged his shoulders. Even that hurt!

"Are you cold?" the lad asked.

That was a foolish question if Finney had ever heard one. Laying on a wooden floor in the cool of night with no clothes on after losing a lot of blood had definitely made him cold. "Yes," he answered in a similar whisper. "I'm freezing."

"Do you want me to cover you with my blanket?"

Finney tried to study the lad's eyes to see if he were genuine, but his orangish-colored bangs partially hid them. That's when Finney noticed how thin the lad was. His arms were semi-muscular but his stomach had not even an inch of flab on it. The cabin was dark, but it appeared the lad's ribcage was visible. Finney didn't know if the kid was ill or malnourished. Regardless of the lad's character or health, Finney knew he would never fall asleep while shivering, so he said, "If you're sure you wouldn't mind, I could use your blanket."

The young man nodded with a smile, "I'll be right back."

As the lad left his side, more tears found their way down Finney's face. This time, instead of tears of sadness, they were tears of pleasant surprise. Somehow, during all of the time he had been sulking, he had forgotten how kind Newt and Cherish had been to him. And now this lad as well. Unlike the Gillcrest plantation, he could make friends here. People he could have intelligent, meaningful conversations with.

It wasn't long before the young man returned and cautiously draped the tip of the blanket over Finney's feet and ankles. Finney groaned.

The lad quickly lifted it back up. "I'm sorry. I didn't mean to hurt you," he whispered.

"I know," Finney replied. "My skin is so torn that anything touching it hurts like you can't imagine."

"I know how it feels. I went through the same thing when I got here last year."

"You did?" Finney asked. "How old were you when you got here?"

"Thirteen."

"That's how old I am now," Finney replied. "Can I ask you something?"

"What's that?"

"Did it make you hate yourself and everybody else here?"

"No," the lad said. "Not at all. I'm the kind of guy who chooses to think myself happy just like the Apostle Paul did."

Finney rolled his eyes. That was the most absurd thing he had ever heard. "You think yourself happy? Like who?"

"Like the Apostle Paul. You know, from the Bible?"

"Oh," Finney said. "You're one of those?"

"If you mean one of those who believe in God, yes, I am. Does that mean you're not?"

"What kind of God would allow people like us to be slaves?" Finney asked.

"The same kind of God who loved us so much that He let His own Son get whipped worse than we did, have nails driven through His hands, and be murdered so we would have a way to go to Heaven. That's what kind of God would allow it."

Finney sighed. "I'm not ready to talk about this right now."

"No problem," the lad said. "When you are, let me know. My name's Kit."

"Sure," Finney said. "You should probably go back to bed though before we wake up the others."

Kit smiled. "Good point. If I wake William up again, he's liable to kill me. Before I lay back down, I have an idea. If I drag that bench over top of you, I could drape the blanket over it so it wouldn't touch your skin, and even though it wouldn't be the same as wrapping up in it, it would at least block some of the night air off of you."

At first, that sounded like a great idea, but only until Finney gave it a little more thought, "That would make too much noise. Dragging that thing over here would wake everybody in the house."

"Do you think you can get over there to it?"

Finney didn't know if he could or not. But it was worth a try. "Help me up," he whispered.

Kit stood to his feet and slightly bent his knees, "Take hold of my arm, and pull yourself up."

Finney grabbed hold with both hands and attempted to pull himself up but felt as though his entire body was going to fall apart as he tried. Grunting and groaning, he whispered, "I can't."

"It's okay," Kit assured him. "But I remember what it was like being in your predicament. You're cold, and you can't stand everybody seeing you naked, right?

Finney grinned, amazed at how well Kit knew him already.

Kit didn't wait for an answer before continuing, "I'm going to stretch the blanket out on the floor. Scoot as far onto it as you can and I'll drag you over to the bench. That'll be a lot quieter than dragging the bench over here."

Getting any part of his body onto that blanket would be rough, but Kit's optimism was contagious. Gritting his teeth, Finney forced himself to army crawl until most of his body was on the blanket.

"Ready?" Kit asked.

"Let's do it."

Using both hands, Kit pulled on the blanket. It worked. In no time, Finney was effortlessly gliding across the floor.

Out of nowhere, Henry rushed over and jumped onto the blanket. "My turn!" the little man exclaimed.

Kit smiled and put a finger to his lips, "Keep your voice down, Henry. We don't want to wake up the others. But you can ride too."

Henry grinned as he wrapped an arm around Finney's neck for support. Finney hissed, and Henry jerked his arm back. "Sorry," he said.

"It's okay," Finney told him. "Anything that touches me hurts. I'm sore all over, buddy. Just hold onto the blanket."

Kit shushed both of them, "You're being too loud. If William gets up, there's going to be quite the ruckus. And if there's a ruckus, Master Levi's gonna blame us. You might as well learn this early on, Finney. William can do no wrong in Master Levi's eyes. For whatever reason, William is the only white nigger the planter seems to like."

Finney still had no idea who William was. But since Kit had already brought up his name twice, and both times in relation to not waking him up, he had a pretty good guess that the fellow liked his sleep and that he had quite the temper. Finney wanted to meet him. Or to at least observe him. If William had found favor with Master Levi, maybe he could too. He'd just have to figure out how William had done it, and follow his footsteps.

After glancing over his shoulder to make sure no one else was stirring, Kit pulled again, a bit slower this time.

"Almost there," he whispered a minute or so later. "Hop off, Henry."

"Why? He's been on longer than me."

"I know," Kit said. "But I could use your help right now. Kit's hurt too bad to get off the blanket on his own and I'm not strong enough to get him off myself. But if you help me with those big muscles of yours, I think we can do it."

Kit had a way with kids, that was for sure. Henry got off that blanket looking as proud as a peacock. "Alright, Finney," Kit spoke softly. "We'll go slow. Try to roll onto your side for us."

That was easier said than done! Finney was afraid to move a muscle. Ever so carefully, and gritting his teeth as he went, he inched himself onto his side, facing away from his helpers.

"Okay, Henry," Kit whispered. "Grab the blanket right here. When I say 'three,' we're going to tug on it with all of our might. Are you ready?"

"Don't worry," Henry said. "I'm strong enough for both of us. I can get it from him."

Finney didn't want to go through with the plan. If that blanket came out from under him too quickly and his body plopped against that floor, he'd likely scream, and then that William fellow would beat, if not kill him outright.

"One," Kit said. Nothing had happened yet, but Finney's pain level was drastically increasing. He didn't want to cry, but how could he not? "Two." Why did they have to do this? Surely, there was a better way! "Three!"

The blanket moved so swiftly, Finney nearly rolled onto his stomach, but he caught himself. Panting heavily, he closed his eyes as Kit and Henry gave it another yank. Before the teenager knew what happened, the blanket was out from under him, and he was able to ease himself back into as comfortable of a position as possible.

"I told you I could do it," Henry said, grinning from ear to ear.

"Good job. Think you can help me get the bench over top of him?"

Henry nodded.

Together, the young men scooted the bench into place.

"Now, let's drape the blanket over him so nobody's eyesight will be ruined by seeing his poop-maker first thing in the morning."

Poop-maker? Finney chuckled for the first time in quite a while. Never had he heard someone's backside referred to in such vulgar terminology. That Kit was something else!

CHAPTER FOUR

REJECTED

One meal per day wasn't going to cut it, no matter what Master Levi Stone said. Had he cared enough to look, he would have seen how skinny, droopy-eyed, and weak all of his white slaves were. How the planter could convince himself or anybody else the smoked Irish and mulatto slaves needed two meals per day while the white niggers only needed one, Finney would never understand.

The hunger pains had faded in the three weeks since the lad's arrival at the Stone plantation, but that did little to ease his mind. He, and the other white slaves, were slowly starving to death. "Why won't you help me?" he asked Kit for the third time.

Kit ripped another clump of weeds out of the ground. "Tell me about your family," he said. "What were they like?"

Finney put on a fake smile, "They were nothing like you, that's for sure."

Without taking as much as a second to think, Kit said, "That's a malicious thing to say about your family."

"What do you mean?"

"If they're the opposite of me," Kit laughed, "that means they're a bunch of whale-sized, revolting as sin, empty-headed fopdoodles. You shouldn't say such things about your relatives."

Raising a shovel full of soil, Finney dumped it over Kit's head. "That dirt'll hide a little of your ugliness. Too bad it didn't have any horse manure mixed in with it, or it might have covered up your foul stench as well."

Kit's face lit up with the kind of smile one would anticipate seeing on a slave who had just acquired his freedom — not when one got covered in dirt. Kit shook his head wildly, sending dirt flying every which direction. Still smiling, he raised his chin, puffed his chest out, and brought his shoulders back. "I'll take that as a compliment, Finney. Not the cover story you used about my odor, of course. But for showering me with dirt to make me look more like one of the mulattos. You were trying to honor me as your superior officer, weren't you?"

Finney smiled. That Kit had a knack for transforming everything into positives. Never would he have come up with such a funny thing to say at a moment's notice. That's not all Kit had a talent for. He had done it again — how could he keep changing the topic so effortlessly?

"Alright, Kit. I've asked you the same question three times, and you keep dodging it like it's dysentery. Why won't you help me sneak into the smoked Irish cabin? They get twice as much as we do."

Kit brought his bottom lip out over his top one and shook his head. "Stealing's not right."

"They did the same thing to you that they did to me. It might be wrong to take from kind people to feed our selfishness. But I'm talking about taking care of our necessities by borrowing from a bunch of brutes who call us white niggers and hunt for every excuse they can find to beat on us. I don't see that as thievery."

Wiping sweat from his brow, Kit said, "That's not who I am, Finney. I can't steal from anybody for any reason. And that's what it is when you borrow from somebody without their permission with no intentions of paying them back. And Finney, all of the smoked Irish aren't our enemies. There are three mulattos who are out to get us. Three, Finney. Why would we hurt an entire cabin full of people because of three bad apples?"

"Okay," Finney replied. "I see where you're coming from. But even if that's the case, every smoked Irish person in that cabin has way more food than we do. I don't need you to steal. Just to help me. All I'm asking you to do is to be my watchman. And to be ready to cause a distraction if need be."

"Finney, do you consider yourself to be my friend?" Kit asked. "Friends don't expect friends to do things that go against their consciences or beliefs. I don't want to fight about this, but I can't have anything to do with your plan."

Friendship isn't always what it's cracked up to be. That's what Darcy always said anyway. Finney let out an irritated sigh, "That's fine. I'll find a way to do it myself."

Kit held the hoe still for a few seconds. "If you do," he replied, "don't share anything you take with me. I meant it when I said I won't have any part of this."

The last thing Finney wanted was to drive a wedge in their friendship. "I get it," he said. "I won't bring it up again. Just promise not to say anything to anybody."

Kit stopped hoeing again. "I won't go out of my way to get you in trouble. But that's something else you should know about me. I don't lie; not to anybody, regardless of the circumstances."

Finney had never met anyone, let alone another teenager, who was such a moral fanatic. Being friends with a prude had never topped Finney's priority list, but it wasn't like he had a garden full of friends to choose from.

Now it was his turn to change the subject. "Who's that one-armed fellow over there that nobody ever talks to?"

Kit looked over. "That's William."

"William? As in the William you're always afraid of waking up?"

"The one and the same. Nobody talks to him because nobody wants to get on his bad side."

Finney didn't get it. Sure, the guy was tall and rather odd looking with his eyebrows practically grown together above his nose and with his overgrown moustache having food crumbs in it and all, but he only had one arm! What could he possibly do to anybody?

"Rumor has it," Kit said after a few seconds of silence, "His own kinfolk trapped him, and sold him into slavery because they were so afraid of him. Then when he came to the new world, they say he lost his arm on another plantation when he got in a fight with a bull."

"With a bull?" Finney asked.

"Said he didn't get enough sleep one night because a cow was making a bunch of noise just outside his cabin. He charged at her, and a bull came to the cow's defense. William didn't take too kindly to that big bull interfering in his fight, so he rushed over and tried to box that thing's ears."

Finney laughed. "You don't actually believe anybody'd be that stupid, do you?"

Kit looked over at William for a second. "Don't call him that," he said.

"What's it to you?"

"Just don't make fun of him. Or anybody else for that matter. It's not right."

"Sorry," Finney said. "Do you think Master Levi likes him on account of the missing arm?"

"I wish I knew," Kit said. "We've all been trying to figure that out ever since Master Levi showed up with him a few months ago."

"Master Levi showed up with him? What do you mean?"

"Every now and then Master Levi takes a trip. He disappears for months at a time. It's only happened twice since I've been here, but they say it's a regular thing. Nobody knows when he's going to leave, where he's going, or when he'll be back. Anyway, the last time he went on such an outing, he left alone and when he returned, William was with him."

"So, Master Levi bought him at an auction?"

"Could have," Kit said. "But I doubt he would have travelled months to go to an auction to buy one slave. I'll tell you another thing that doesn't make any sense.

William's the only white nigger here that doesn't have Master Levi's initials burned into his flesh. I got branded my first day here, and so did you. Why would he be any different?"

"I don't know," Finney said. Maybe Master Levi felt like on account of his missing arm, he'd already been through enough? But we could make guesses about that all day. But that comment you made about your first day got me thinking. You've not said much about your arrival here. Was it just like mine?"

"Mostly," Kit said. "But two days are never exactly alike."

"Well, what were the differences?"

"I don't know."

"Tell me the whole story then, from the time you woke up that morning, until you went to bed that night."

"Why?"

"I don't know. I'm just curious. That's all."

"The first thing I remember from that day? Let me think. The man chained next to me on the ship and I were both praying out loud, as we had heard we were arriving at the colonies. We prayed that if it were in God's will, we would be purchased by the same person."

"Is that man here?" Finney asked.

"No. It must not have been meant to be."

Finney wasn't surprised. How did so many people believe in a God who wouldn't give them what they asked for?

"Anyway," Kit went on, "The shipmaster ordered his crew to take us out of the hold. The ship was coming to a stop as we arrived on deck, and what looked like hundreds of planters were lined up, waiting to board.

The shipmaster lined all of us up, and said something along the lines of, 'Welcome to your new life in the colonies. Obey each of the folks who board this ship, keeping in mind that any of them could become your new master. You don't want to upset anyone here. If you cause a ruckus, I won't hesitate to tear your flesh before, during, or after the auction. I expect each of you to be polite and to follow every instruction you're given.' He then turned to one of his crew members and said, 'Let them board. They've got three hours to examine the merchandise prior to placing their bids.''

"They didn't bathe you all or make you clean the ship before the buyers got on board?"

"No," Kit replied. "I think the shipmaster was too afraid of mutiny to have us unchained long enough to clean anything. We were all filthy dirty and smelled fouler than anything I had ever smelled in my life. That didn't seem to discourage the buyers though. They poked and prodded and questioned all of us for what seemed like an eternity. Eventually, they opened things up for bidding. Master Levi was the only one who bid on me. It seemed everybody else received multiple bids. But for whatever reason, I was the least favorite candidate of all those up for auction."

"I'm sure you weren't the only one who didn't receive multiple bids," Finney said.

"You might be right," Kit replied. "I just know that most of the people around me were bid on by multiple buyers, and I wasn't."

"Were you the only slave Master Levi purchased that day?"

"He purchased three of us. But one of the others got sick and died shortly after arriving here. The other one was here for a few months, but Master Levi sold her off. Nobody ever told us why. We didn't see her rebel or slack off on her work. Maybe he just didn't like her."

"What happened to the three of you when you got here?"

"Well, pretty much the same thing that happened to you. The girl was the first one they broke in. Achan led her over to Master Levi, who burned his initials into her right arm. Immediately afterward, Duncan grabbed her left wrist, while she was still screaming out in pain, and dragged her to the whipping post. Achan took the lad in front of me over to Master Levi, who tugged his breeches down and burned his initials into his behind. Duncan was in the process of stripping the girl and securing her to the whipping post, so Achan ordered the young man to drop to his knees and remain there until Duncan had taught the girl a lesson. Then, of course, it was my turn. Achan grabbed my arm and marched me over to Master Levi. I remember hoping with everything in me that he would just brand my arm like he did the girl's. But no. He jerked my breeches down and pressed that branding iron tight against my behind. I've since learned that's the way it's always done. The girls get it on the arm, whereas the lads get it on the backside. Achan ordered me to join the other lad on my knees just as Duncan began viciously whipping that poor girl. She begged and pleaded for him to stop. The sights and sounds of what she was going through made me think far less about how badly my bottom was burning and about the torture that was yet to come. Achan stayed with me and the other lad while Master Levi walked over to supervise the lashing."

It was too soon. Finney should not have asked to hear Kit's story. Not yet. Suddenly, his heart began racing. His entire body broke out in a cold sweat. Never would he forget what they did to him on his first day. He felt like he was about to experience the whole thing all over again. "That's enough," he said. "I don't want to hear anymore."

Kit looked surprised. "I thought you wanted to know about everything from the moment I got up until the time I went to bed."

"I thought I did, but I can't handle it. It's far too much far too soon."

CHAPTER FIVE

EYE OPENER

Slaves of every color would soon be back to their shacks, and there wasn't a second to lose. After triple-checking his surroundings to make sure no one was watching, Finney rushed inside. The smoked Irish shack was nearly identical to his, except that the white nigger cabin was far less tidy. Finney hurried to the cupboards, finding them every bit as poorly stocked as he had suspected.

A pathetic amount of rice, a potato, and an ear of maize would be all Finney could swipe without getting busted. Stuffing his pockets, the hungry, vengeful thief rushed out of the shack. Thankfully he saw, nor heard anyone coming. Running to the woodshed, he stashed the food behind a pile of scrap lumber before making a mad dash to the white nigger cabin.

Kit met him at the door. Nobody else was there yet. "Did you go through with it?"

"I did," Finney smiled as the two walked inside. "Why? Did you change your mind?"

Kit closed his eyes, "No. I was hoping you did."

"Not a chance," Finney said, taking a seat next to the table. "You sure you don't want to sneak out and eat with me tonight? I'll wait till everybody's sound asleep before making my move."

Joining him at the table, Kit shook his head, "Thanks for the offer. But I don't think so. We better talk about something else. I hear them coming."

Kit was right. It sounded like they were just outside the cabin. Oh, how he hoped no one had overheard! A change of subject was necessary. But what else was there to talk about?

Thankfully, Kit had him covered. "I just can't get over how good God is to us," he said. "Every time we wake up, it's only because He allows us to."

Finney didn't know what to say, but he didn't have to. Newt was coming through the door with Henry latching onto his hand. "I sure wish I had the energy of you lads," Newt said. "Both of you disappeared faster than a flash of lightning. Was there a reason for the hurry?"

"No, sir," Finney said, shaking his head while swatting at and barely missing a fly on the table. "We just felt like running. That's all."

Newt gave the lads a questioning look. "Kit, I know you a lot better than I know Finney here. I'm not saying Finney's dishonest but be careful who you buddy up with. I'd hate to see you fall into mischief."

What kind of mixed-up statement was that? If Newt didn't think Finney was dishonest, he would have no reason to warn Kit to be cautious about who he befriended. Who did Newt think he was? The judge of all truths?

Henry wouldn't allow Finney to stay mad for long. Letting go of his father's hand, he asked, "Who is Miss Chiff? And why would anybody fall into her?"

Finney wanted to laugh, but didn't want to hurt Henry's feelings. The way kids understood things could be absolutely hilarious!

With a slight chuckle, Newt gently corrected the lad, "Not Miss Chiff. Mischief. It's a word that means trouble. I was warning Kit to be careful not to fall into trouble. Got it?

"Fall into trouble? I've fallen in the creek before. But how do you fall into trouble?"

Finney and Kit smiled at each other as Newt said, "It's a figure of speech, son. Don't worry about it."

"I'm not worrying about it," Henry replied. "I just want to know what it means."

Newt chuckled a little harder than before.

Finney couldn't blame him. More than likely, Henry wouldn't understand any explanation his father could give him. If he were Newt, he would have ended the conversation right there.

But Newt had a plan. "Okay, little man," he said. "Close your eyes and imagine you're walking along the river bank."

Henry not only closed, but covered his eyes with both hands.

"Can you picture it?" Newt asked.

"Yes, sir," Henry said. "I sure can. And guess what just happened?"

Shaking his head, Newt asked, "What's that?"

"A giant fish with whiskers jumped out of the water, stuck out his tongue, and caught a mosquito."

Finney laughed at that one. Henry was a lot like his little sister, Boann. That sounded like something she would have said. Oh, how he missed that girl!

"He did?" Newt continued, "That's something right there! Alright, keep those eyes closed for me. As you're walking along that bank and that jumping fish catches your attention, you don't see that the bank's washed out right in front of you. You keep walking straight ahead as you have been, and *splash!* Into the water you go!"

"Do I get hurt?" Henry asked.

Finney and Newt exchanged grins. "Yes," Newt said. "You scrape your knees because you aren't paying attention to what's going on around you. Okay, open your eyes."

"I don't want to open them," Henry said.

"And why is that, son?"

"I don't want to see the blood."

Newt laughed. "Henry, it was a story. It didn't really happen."

Henry looked up, "So you lied?"

Finney couldn't do anything to keep a grin off his face. After all, the lad did have a point. But what was it Darcy always said? Oh, yes! Never interfere in another family's debate. That was so much easier said than done! But, if he set his mind to it, he could keep his mouth shut.

"No, Henry," Newt said. "I didn't lie. I just wanted you to picture something."

"But Momma told me last week that whenever I say something that's not true, it's a lie. Did you say I scraped my knees?"

"Yes, but I—"

"But I didn't really scrape them. So that's a lie."

Finney's insides were in knots. He couldn't wait to hear how Newt would attempt to talk himself out of this one! Henry may have been young, but his thought process was quite logical — at least for the moment.

"A lie, Henry, is when a person tries to convince another person something is true, when it's not."

"Like convincing me I fell into the water when I didn't?"

Newt threw a hand high in the air and laughed, "What am I going to do with you, child?"

"It isn't funny to lie. If I tell Momma what you did, she might take a switch to you."

Now that Finney wanted to see! He could picture it now. Cherish chasing after Newt with a giant switch in hand. Him yelling at her to calm down. Her swinging that thing with everything she had in her. Him yelping as she lit into him. Now that would be a scene nobody on that plantation would soon forget!

"Your momma's not going to take a switch to me," Newt said. "I don't think you really understand the difference between a lie and using your imagination."

"I understand," Henry said. "When kids tell stories that aren't true, it's lies but when adults do the same thing, it's called using their imaginations."

Everybody but Henry fought to keep themselves from laughing. How could the lad be so serious? Had he been any older, he would have been the one having a switch taken to him. Oh, how nice it must be to be Henry's age!

Cherish walked through the door, kicking an apple core out of her way, and was taken back by the amused expressions on everyone's faces. "What did I miss?" she asked.

"Henry," Newt replied.

"That's all you have to say," Cherish giggled. Plopping down next to Kit, she placed her hands on the back of her neck and looked toward the ceiling. Letting out a yawn, she said, "Am I the only one who feels like sleeping right now? I am worn out!"

"I'm with ya, darlin'," Newt said. "And there's nobody I'd rather sleep next to than you."

Finney's parents had never spoken so sweetly to one another. At the Gillcrest plantation, he had seen a little bit of kindness between Jonah and his wife. But there was something different about Newt and Cherish's relationship. Not only with each other, but even with how they related to Henry.

It wasn't only their family either. There was something different about Kit too. It was like some of the folks he shared that cabin with her naïve. Like they didn't realize they were slaves, or how bad they had it. Finney wished he could somehow see things through their eyes.

Unfortunately, everybody in the cabin didn't have the same mindset. Two women barged through the door, bickering.

"I did not!" one of them shouted.

"Lie, lie, lie! That's all you do! You're a liar, Jane, and everybody knows it!!"

Jane stepped closer to the other girl. Finney couldn't help but stare at her flaring nostrils. Whatever was going on between the two of them must have been serious. Neither of the ladies came across as being willing to back down from the other. Somebody was about to get slapped.

Raising and shaking both arms, palms flipped upwards, Jane yelled, "What makes you think I'm lyin'?"

"Really? You wouldn't know the truth if it smacked you upside the face. Every time your mouth moves, you lie!"

It wasn't going to be long. Somebody was about to get hurt. Finney watched Newt and Cherish to see if either were going to break it up. Somebody sure needed to.

"If you said something that's not true—" Henry tried to interrupt before Newt covered his mouth.

Cherish jumped up and stormed over to the women, "Harriet, Jane, you two stop all of this squabbling right now! You are both grown adults. Stop setting such horrible examples for the children."

Crossing her arms and jutting her bottom lip out, Harriet turned and faced the wall. Jane, on the other hand, said, "Nobody invited you into our business. This is between us."

Newt stood up, and unless Finney was hearing things, he growled as he did so. "You made it our business when you took part in this shouting match in the presence of our little boy. If you don't want us involved, settle your differences outside!"

Harriet looked at Newt and then glanced at Henry. She looked as though she felt guilty for how she'd behaved.

Jane, not so much. "Let me tell you what happened. She—"

Cherish shook her head, "No. We have heard all we're going to hear. Either close your mouths or go outside.

This is our home, and a home is supposed to be a place of rest."

CHAPTER SIX

THE
MISUNDERSTANDING

Kit and Finney sat on the ground with their backs against the wall, devouring the small portion of eggs Cherish gave them for breakfast. Finney didn't understand how the others did it. Had he not been regularly stealing food, he wouldn't have been able to survive on that one tiny meal per day.

Glancing at Finney's stomach, Kit said, "You've got to stop. It's obvious you're putting on more weight than the rest of us. Master Levi's not the kind of planter who will allow thievery to go unpunished. Neither are his mulattos. They don't let us crackers get away with anything. Why do you think I haven't hightailed it yet?

"Thinkin' of running away, are you now, you filthy white nigger?" Achan asked, rounding the corner of the cabin. Finney nearly swallowed his tongue. Of all people to happen by, why did it have to be a mulatto?

"Na, no, sir," Kit stammered.

Achan turned and focused his dark, evil eyes on Finney, "So it was your friend here planning to sneak off?"

"No, sir," both lads said in unison.

"What was all that talk about runnin' away then?"

Kit stood up, "I was telling Finney that Master Levi is a very strict master, and—"

"Oh," Achan laughed. "I see. So, you were speaking poorly of Master Levi?"

"No," Kit insisted. "I was simply tellin' him this isn't the kind of plantation where a white slave should ever expect to get away with anything."

"So, you were saying the master treats his smoked Irish better than his white niggers? Come with me, cracker. We're gonna see how Master Levi wants to address this situation."

Finney wanted to rush to Kit's defense, but he didn't know what to say. It wasn't like he could do anything to prevent Achan or Master Levi from whipping him. If anything, speaking up would probably get both lads into deeper trouble.

As Kit left with Achan, Finney had flashbacks to his initiation. He could still hear the mulattos excitedly laughing as his flesh was being torn open. He flinched as he felt that branding iron searing his backside.

Here it was, only a few short weeks after his own lashing and his only friend on the property looked as though he were about to suffer a similar fate. If it were going to happen, Finney certainly hoped it would take place where he wouldn't have to watch.

Less than fifteen minutes later, just as the slaves were heading out to work the tobacco crops, the planter made an announcement. "Before you hit the fields, I need your attention. Come this way."

Even though he was growing accustomed to Master Levi's voice, for a split-second Finney thought it was Uncle Keir calling out. How those men could look so much alike yet be entirely different people remained a mystery to him.

Turning and walking toward the voice, Finney couldn't help but stare at Master Levi. His new master was the same height, of an extremely similar build, wore the same hairstyle, and had the same face as his uncle. Maybe they were twins?

Ahead, he could see Master Levi and his three mulatto overseers holding Kit while tying his hands and wrists together. By the time Finney and the other slaves caught up to them, Kit was being hoisted into the air, arms stretched high above his head. At least he still had his clothes on and Master Levi wasn't holding a whip.

As the slaves approached, Master Levi said, "Folks, we'll make this quick as there's much work to be done. This white nigger has confessed to speaking poorly of me, his master, as well as to entertaining thoughts of running away. Neither of which am I willing to tolerate."

The planter poked a stick in the fire. "Raise the cracker four feet higher," he ordered.

Finney wasn't sure what was about to happen, but it didn't look good. At first, he thought Master Levi might be planning to whip him with the hot stick. But that didn't make sense on account of Kit still being fully clothed.

Duncan and Achan pulled the rope back further, raising Kit entirely off the ground. The lad let out a painful cry as the ropes cut into him. The men pulled, stopped, and pulled again. Each time they started and stopped, another pain-filled groan or scream filled Finney's ears.

"That's good," Master Levi said, pulling the blazing stick out of the fire. "You'll remember this day for the rest of your life, red-leg."

Not wanting to see whatever was coming, Finney closed his eyes, only to have Cuddy smack him on the back of the head. "Open those eyes, unless you want to join him!"

It was difficult, but Finney forced himself to not only open his eyes but to keep them that way.

The planter moved the fiery branch to about six inches beneath Kit's feet. Kit pulled his feet higher, amusing Master Levi and half of the mulattos.

"Whew! Yeah!" Cuddy shouted.

"That'll teach him," Duncan joined in.

Master Levi raised the new weapon of cruelty even higher. The more he raised it, the more Kit attempted to elevate his legs, all the while screaming, "I wasn't going to run away! I won't ever run! Pleeeaasseee sssttttoooppp! It burns! It burns! It burns!"

Kit had his legs tucked as high as he could get them. "Noooo! It burns! Noooo!" he screamed as the planter brought the fire closer to his feet.

Finney closed his eyes and gritted his teeth. Cuddy smacked him again, "Keep those eyes open, you filthy white nigger."

If Finney weren't so mortified by what was taking place right in front of him, he'd have returned the favor. Those mulattos had no right to rough him up. Why Master Levi made the mulattos overseers in the first place made no sense.

It didn't matter. The planter was torturing an innocent lad in front of at least fifty or sixty witnesses, and nobody was stepping up to his defense. While some of the onlookers obviously thought Kit deserved it, others appeared as upset as Finney was.

Kit's feet were beginning to smoke, and his screaming was becoming unbearable. His body flailed around like crazy as his feet were scorched.

Master Levi pulled the branch away, but Kit's screaming and crying was far from over.

Master Levi grounded the fiery end of the limb into the dirt before him. "Rebellious acts will be dealt with harshly. None of you dare cross me again!"

CHAPTER SEVEN

FURIOUS

Watching Kit alternate between crawling on all fours and scooting on his bottom to work for the very people who had injured him was infuriating. Every time the lad winced or whined, Finney mentally replayed what Master Levi had done to him. He'd like to see that planter strung up by his hands and have his feet charred. Better yet, to have him tied up by his toes and have his head scorched.

"Can I ask you something, Kit?" the lad asked after working in silence for nearly two hours.

"Sure."

Finney was afraid Kit might say that. Some things are easier to think about than to say out loud. "You said you've been on this plantation since sometime last year, right?"

"Right," Kit said.

"So, you probably know a lot about Master Levi?"

"I suppose," Kit said again with a playful smile.

Finney didn't understand what Kit found funny about giving such short answers. It was as if the lad didn't take anything seriously. Even if Kit wasn't going to make things easier for him, he had to ask, "Do you happen to know if he has a twin brother?"

Kit stopped working, and his grin faded just as quickly as it had appeared. "A twin?" he repeated. "Not that I know of. Why do you ask?"

Finally, an answer that consisted of more than two words! The only problem was, Kit's tone changed a little too quickly. Why did he suddenly become so serious? Was there something Kit didn't want him to know?

"Finney, are you still with me? Why were you asking if Master Levi has a twin?"

Finney's stomach churned. Perhaps he shouldn't have brought his suspicions to light. But now that he had, there was no turning back. "I know this is going to sound ridiculous," he said, "but Master Levi looks, sounds, and even carries himself like my uncle. I keep thinking they have to be related somehow."

Kit smiled again, this time a bit mischievously, "Master Levi looks like your uncle? And where does your uncle live, Finney?"

That was a fair question, though it didn't necessarily need to be asked. Still, if Finney wanted Kit to answer his questions, he would have to return the favor. "The last time I saw Uncle Keir, he was living in Dublin. But I haven't seen him for years. Where he lives, or where he lived doesn't change the fact that Uncle Keir and Master Levi have a lot of similarities. Even though I asked if

Master Levi has a twin, I can't help but think Master Levi and Uncle Keir might be the same person."

"They might be," Kit scoffed. "You don't think you could positively identify your own uncle?"

"That's why I'm so confused. I'm nearly certain I recognize him, but if he's Uncle Keir, why doesn't he recognize me? Or is he only pretending not to know who I am? You know, like, maybe he's ashamed of the double-life he's living or something?"

Kit's grin grew wider, stretching nearly from ear to ear, although he didn't say a word. "What?" Finney asked. "What's that look for?"

Kit shook his head, "Wow! Being related to Master Levi could be considered a blessing. Then again, it could be a curse."

"I understand the blessing part, but how could it be a curse?"

"Don't worry about it, Finney. There are a lot of people out there who look like each other. I, for one, don't think Master Levi is your uncle."

Regardless of what Kit thought, Finney was of another persuasion. Even if Master Levi wasn't Uncle Keir, but was only his twin brother, that would still make them kin. And if the planter knew they were related, perhaps he'd set the lad free? But to suggest such a thing without any proof of kinship to a man whose heart was about as tender as a crocodile's didn't seem like the best idea Finney had ever had. But if he had evidence, it would be a different story altogether.

A pile of dirt kissed Finney's face. The lad shook his head while giving Kit a confused look.

"Oh, good. You are still with me," Kit teased. "I've been talking to you for over five minutes and you haven't heard a word I've said."

"You were not."

"I was," Kit insisted. "You were in a world all of your own. So, what were you really going to ask me about?"

Finney had done such a great job of changing the subject, he'd nearly forgotten what he started to ask to begin with. With Kit's question jogging his memory, he would have to think fast. Perhaps this wasn't the best time to have that conversation.

The lad pretended he had no idea what Kit was talking about. "What do you mean?" he asked.

"You know what I mean. You weren't going to ask me about Master Levi. There was something else on your mind. Something heavier. I sensed it."

Finney rubbed his hands on his breeches before stretching his fingers a few times.

"Something's bothering you," Kit continued. "Did I do something to upset you?"

Finney shook his head. "Don't worry about it," he said, pulling out a clump of weeds while looking across the field just in time to catch a glimpse of Henry tripping over his mother's skirt and falling on his chin. "Ow," Henry exclaimed loudly, "I hurt my hand." Cherish kept working as if nothing had happened.

Finney chuckled. If he ever had a son one day, he hoped he was a lot like that little fellow.

"What's on your mind, Finney? You know I'm not going to let it go. You might as well tell me."

It's not that Finney didn't want to talk about it. It was more that he didn't want to come across as rude or ignorant. But if he knew Kit as well as he thought he did, Kit was going to drag it out of him eventually. Finney decided he might as well make things easier on himself. "It's about *God*," he said, pausing to see how his friend would react.

Kit turned to make eye contact, "What about Him?"

"I don't understand. You obey God so He won't be angry with you, right? That's why you won't take anybody else's food even when you know your body needs it? And why you won't accept any I've taken?"

"Right," Kit nodded.

Finney shook his head while yanking out another clump of weeds. Believers have some weird ideas. Perhaps somebody needed to come right out and tell them that. And what good are friends if they don't tell you when you're wrong? That's what Darcy always said anyway. "*If* God is real, and He honors obedience, how come *I* haven't gotten punished for taking the food, but *you* took an extreme punishment when you didn't do anything wrong?"

Kit flipped a long, weird looking black bug off his knee. "Promise not to get mad or offended with my answer?"

"I promise," Finney said, shaking dirt out of an enormous clump of weed roots.

"The reason God's not dealing with you for stealing is that you're not His child. God punishes His children more than He punishes the devil's."

How could Kit say such a thing with a straight face? That lad wasn't right in the head; he couldn't be. Finney chuckled sarcastically. "So now I'm a child of the devil?"

"Sorry to say it, but yes," Kit agreed. "As is everybody who's not saved."

"Okay, I'll play along. I'm the devil's son, and you're God's. Why did God allow you to get unjustly punished and me to get away with stealing?"

Kit glanced at his sore, badly burnt feet before returning his gaze to meet Finney's. "Am I really innocent? Didn't I have thoughts about running away? I'm not saying I deserved to have my feet set afire for that, but I'm not going to be upset over it either. God has a reason for everything."

"God has a reason? Kit, you probably won't be able to walk for a long time. And God didn't do anything to protect you. You're still going to defend Him?"

Obviously uncomfortable, Kit turned and began weeding again. "I'm still alive, and still have my health," he said. "God knows what He's doing, and I trust Him."

"Yeah, and I trust Master Levi and the mulattos too," Finney grumbled sarcastically.

Kit let out a sigh.

"What is that supposed to mean?"

"I don't know what to think or do right now, Finney. I like you and all, but I don't know how long I can be friends with somebody who thinks so poorly of God. Especially if that person is going out of their way to shake my faith."

That Kit sure took his beliefs seriously! Apparently, he was one of those hypocrites Finney's parents had often complained about. He might as well have said, "Don't get offended at my answer, but I'll get offended when you respond." Who needs that kind of friend anyway? If Kit wanted to be foolish enough to choose his invisible God, who had let him suffer for doing good instead of having a friend he could see and talk to, that was his decision.

Through squinted eyes, Finney glanced over to see if Kit was working; he wasn't. The lad was sitting on his knees with his head bowed and his eyes closed. His lips were moving, but no words were coming out and a tear was trickling down his cheek.

Shaking his head, Finney turned to face the opposite direction and resumed weeding the field.

CHAPTER EIGHT

GIRL FIGHT

Fights on the Stone plantation were rare, but when one occurred, it was a doozy. This one was different being that it was Jane, a white cracker, and a smoked Irish slave Finney hadn't yet met. Finney hadn't heard any arguing, so he wasn't sure how the fight started, but those girls were going at it! Jane pinned the smoked Irish girl tight against a tree and repeatedly slapped her face until she fell to the ground.

As soon as Jane turned her back to walk away, the smoked Irish girl hopped up, charged at her, jumped on her back, and wrapped an arm around her neck. Jane took several giant steps backward and tried to crush her opponent against a tree. Around and around, they went.

The mulattos watched the fight, but did nothing to stop them. That is until one of them saw Master Levi heading in their direction. "Break it up, girls. Now!" he ordered. "Get back to work. We don't have time for foolishness."

Jane smirked, "Fine by me," she said. "I know where Phoebe sleeps."

Phoebe rolled her eyes. "I hope vu don't zink zat scares me. Arh! Try hanzying tonight, and vu von't liffe to zee tomorrow."

What a response! That Phoebe may not have pronounced her words properly, but she had no trouble getting her point across.

First, Jane and Harriet. Now, Jane and Phoebe. Darcy always said if a person has trouble getting along with everybody around them, everybody else isn't at fault. Finney didn't have to know anything about Phoebe to know she was most likely in the right. But even if she had somehow started the skirmish, he liked that fiery spirit Phoebe had. If the two of them were to buddy up, they would be unstoppable. But befriending someone he was supposed to have little to no contact with would be challenging.

Finney would make it happen. How, he didn't yet know. But unless he was out of his mind, Phoebe needed to become a part of whatever plan he developed to regain his freedom.

Getting closer, Master Levi growled, "What was all of that commotion about?"

"I'm sorry, Master Levi," Achan said. "It wasn't anybody's intention to disturb you. A couple of ladies were entertaining us by yanking each other's hair out."

Master Levi glared at the girls for a moment. "You," he said, pointing at Phoebe. "You're the troublemaker. I see it in your eyes."

Finney didn't know what Master Levi saw in her eyes, but it wasn't the same thing he saw. Phoebe looked like the innocent victim who had done nothing more than stand up for herself.

Finney wasn't the only one who saw it that way. "Me? Ein trouplemaker?" Phoebe asked. "Efferypody here knovs petder zan zat. Put I really don't care. If peating me vill make vu feel petter apout yourself, chust ko right ahead und do it. If I liffe, vonderful. If I die, zo pe it. Vu know good and vell zat zee only reazon vu're binning zis on me is—"

"Come with me," Master Levi cut her off, "and we'll see to it you don't cause any more problems. And you, young lady," he said, locking his eyes on Jane, "you better get on task."

Jane nodded, "Yes, Master Levi. I should have just wiped her spit off my face and continued working. I was wrong to not overlook it."

Phoebe, without hesitation, charged toward Jane, but Master Levi stuck his foot out and tripped her. As soon as she hit the ground, he set a foot in the middle of her back. "Thank you for proving my point." Master Levi turned his attention to Achan, "If there's any more *entertainment* out here, Achan, I'll hold you personally responsible. Get everybody back to work. Now!"

"Yes, sir, Master Levi," Achan said before turning to the other slaves. "You all heard Master Levi, right? Enough time's been wasted away today. Get to laboring before I get to whippin'! Got me?" He glared at Finney. "What are you looking at, cracker? You volunteering to go first?"

Knowing he had done nothing wrong and how hard the mulattos strove to find excuses to whip the white slaves, Finney said, "No, sir. I was listening to you. But I'm getting to work now."

Master Levi grinned, "Achan, I knew I could count on you. Don't disappoint me."

"I won't let you down, sir."

Finney dug a handful of small stones out of the soil before him while worrying what might happen to Phoebe. He hadn't seen how the fight started, but from what he'd previously seen of Jane, he somehow doubted Phoebe was to blame for their skirmish. If she really spat on Jane, he was certain Jane had asked for it.

As Master Levi and Phoebe disappeared from sight, Finney wondered what Phoebe had gone through to make her so bitter. How long had she been a slave? More importantly, would she be interested in helping him plan a revolt?

Kit interrupted his train of thought. Approaching Finney on his knees, he said, "I wish we could find a way to mend our differences."

Finney shook his head, "You're the one who built the wall. Did you forget that?"

Kit put his hands on the ground and crawled closer. "You insulted my Father. How did you expect me to react?"

"Pardon me. Did you forget that you referred to me as a child of the devil?"

Achan stormed over, whip in hand, "What part of 'Get to laboring' did you white niggers not understand? There ain't no time for talkin'. This is your final warning. Shush and keep those hands movin.'"

"Yes, sir," Finney said.

"Sorry, sir," Kit added.

A high-pitched terror-stricken scream rang out from the direction Master Levi and Phoebe had headed out in. That scream was followed up by several more. Finney didn't know what Master Levi was doing to teach Phoebe a lesson. He wasn't even sure he wanted to know. But he sure hoped that screaming would stop sooner rather than later.

CHAPTER NINE

NIGHT MEETING

Coming out of the outhouse, Finney saw her. At least he thought it was her anyway. But why would Phoebe be wandering around so late at night, still wearing the same clothes she had worked and fought in? Maybe she was planning an escape of her own?

The smoked Irish looked right at Finney. He was certain she saw him. Without warning, she spun around and marched off in the opposite direction. "Wait!" Finney whispered loudly.

Phoebe walked faster.

Sprinting toward her, the lad called out again, slightly louder than before, "Phoebe! Stop. I want to talk to you."

Phoebe broke into a jog, which quickly grew into a full-fledged run.

"Why are you running?" Finney called out, still trailing her. "I'm not going to hurt you! Please stop!"

Phoebe ran several more steps before coming to an abrupt halt. Turning to face him, she asked, "Vat do vu vant vith me?"

Grabbing his side, Finney said, "Thanks for stopping. I just wanted to tell you how sorry I am for what happened today. Not only for the fight but for how Master Levi treated you afterward."

"Does telling me how zorry vu are zomehow make vu feel petder apout yourself?"

Finney shook his head. "No. I just don't think what they did to you is right, and I thought you should know."

"Vell, zanks for telling me. Can I ko now?"

"You don't need permission from me," Finney said. "I'm a slave just like you are. I can't do anything to stop you from going if that's what you want to do. But if you're not in a hurry, I thought maybe we could talk. Could you use a friend?"

"Ein friend? Vat makes vu zink I vould vant to pe friends vith ein vite cracker?"

That explained everything! Here Finney had been wondering how his apology could have been taken so wrong. It wasn't because he had said or done anything to give her the wrong idea. She wanted nothing to do with him because he was a cracker. Well, there was nothing he could do about how he was born. If that's the way she felt, it would be impossible to build a friendship with her. For that matter, what was the point of even talking to someone of such a superior skin tone?

"Never mind," the lad said. "I'll just head back to the white nigger cabin and leave you alone." With that, he walked around her and headed toward his cabin. Maybe there was more to it than the color of his skin. Maybe

Phoebe could see a resemblance between him and Master Levi. If that were the case, he could understand why she didn't like him.

Before the lad had time to fully dive into that train of thought, Phoebe ran up beside him. "Vu don't take chokes fery vell, do vu?"

"I didn't hear any jokes."

Phoebe giggled, "Let me sdart offer zen. Ja, I vould loffe to pe your friend. It abears vu halready know mein name is Bhoebe. Vat is yours?"

Finney stopped dead in his tracks, not sure what to think. Had the girl really been joking with him? Or did she suddenly feel guilty for what she had said? Perhaps she was just waiting for him to share his name and then she'd hurl another insult of some kind at him. The last thing he wanted was to involve himself in a bickering match right before bed. That would only make for a long night of unnecessary tossing and turning. But if he didn't take the time to find out her true motive, he'd still pass the night tossing and turning, wondering what might have happened had he heard her out.

After giving the matter a moment or two of thought, he said, "You sure you don't mind that I'm just a cracker?"

Phoebe smiled, "I vas teasing. I bromize."

According to the girl's eyes, she was telling the truth; the lad was certain of it. "In that case, I'm Finney," he said.

Phoebe gave him a blank look. Not sure what to make of it, Finney continued, "So, obviously I was out here to use the outhouse. Why were you out here so late if you don't mind my asking?"

"I vas doing vat I do pest. Zearching for hansvers zat don't zeem to exist."

Finney didn't know what kind of response he had expected, but that wasn't it. How exactly does a person search for answers by wandering around aimlessly under the cover of darkness? Finney doubted she was telling the truth. More than likely, his original suspicion had been right. She was searching for something alright — a way off the plantation. But he could never come right out and accuse her of such a thing. Instead, he decided to play along. "What kind of answers are you looking for?"

"I vant to hunderstand vy I'm here. Vy vas I porn? Vy couldn't I schtay vith mein barents? Vy did I haffe to pecome ein slaffe? Vy am I plack? Vy, out of all zee blaces I could haffe peen but, did I end up on zee Sdone blantazion? Vat is zee boint of mein hexidence? Zere are zo many gueszions, put nein hansvers."

Finney could relate. He had asked himself most of those same questions plenty of times since leaving Dublin. But he still had no clue what she meant about searching for answers. What did she think? They were hiding under a rock? Or in a tree? Or that the wind was going to whisper something in her ear if she walked by herself long enough? Phoebe was either lying about her activities or she was just an odd individual. Either way, Finney wanted to keep the conversation going so he asked, "How long have you been walking around out here anyway?"

"Zis time, maype ein hour. I come out here hanydime I can't sleep. I look up at zee moon und zee sdars, lisden to zee vind, preathe in zat cool night air. All zee vile, I vait and hobe to hunderstand zis crasy vorld ve liffe in. Tonight, mein mind is reeling effen more zan normal zough afder zee fight. I don't mean to rample zo much. Put vu asked if I need ein friend. Now vu brobably hundersdand vy I don't haffe any."

"Yeah. I get it. As much as you talk, I don't think we can be friends."

"Are vu zerious?"

"Of course not," Finney chuckled. "I was simply returning the favor. So what was that fight all about anyway?"

"Oh, zat boor vite nigger — oh, I'm zorry! I mean, chane chust gets on mein nerffes. Effery time I zee her, I feel like placking her eyes und knocking her teeth out. I keep looking for ein excuze to do it, und totay sche kaffe me one."

That Phoebe! She definitely had some grit! "What did she do?"

"Sche looked right at me und pelched on her vay py. Sche did it on burpoze. Chust to make me mad. Zo, I kaffe her vat sche vanded. I kot mad. Und sche kot vat sche had coming to her. I don't care if Masder Leffi agrees or not. I did vat neeted to pe done, und I would do it akain in ein heartpeat."

"I don't understand. Jane belched in your direction. I'm sure it was gross, and probably smelled horrible. If you had ignored it and walked on by, nothing else would have happened to you. But because you decided to punch her, you both ended up with scrapes and bruises. And then Master Levi gave you a beating for it. I would think it would make more sense to ignore the belch to avoid being tortured."

"Oh, vu heard zat screaming?" Phoebe giggled awkwardly. "Vell, zee vip did not feel fery kood. I admit zat. Put I vould take hanozer vibing any day if it meant I had ein hobordunity to teach zat girl ein lezon."

Finney was thankful he stopped Phoebe. The more he talked to her, the more he knew she was just the friend he needed in his life. In time, as they got to know and trust one another more, they could make a plan to get off of that plantation, or possibly even lead a slave uprising. If there was one person on that property who could help him pull it off, it was Phoebe.

CHAPTER TEN

TEAMING UP

Darcy always said wicked deeds refuse to be lonely. Perhaps that's why Finney did it. Not that he considered taking the food he needed for survival to be a wicked deed.

There was the signal! Phoebe could make the perfect whip-poor-will call. Finney made his way out of the bushes, and the two of them slipped into the woodshed. "Where are you getting the extra food from again?" she asked.

Finney wasn't about to tell his new friend he was stealing it out of her cabin. Somehow, he doubted that would go over very well. "From Master Levi's house," he lied.

Phoebe smiled mischievously. "How long haffe vu peen getding avay vith zis?"

"I don't know. Maybe a month?"

"It's apout time zey prought zomepody to zis blantazion vo isn't afraid to pe ein risk-taker."

That was the type of response Finney had hoped for. It was nice to find somebody on the plantation who actually had a brain and wasn't too yellow to take chances or to support others who did. Finney unloaded his pockets. Two potatoes, and a mound of beans may not have been a lot, but they would have to do.

Phoebe smiled. "Is zat all vu kot?" She pulled out a container of blackberries. "Here, I prought dezert."

Finney couldn't believe his eyes. "Where did you get those?"

"Zee zame blace vu kot zee botatoes und peans! Great minds zink alike, huh?"

Finney couldn't help but chuckle. That girl had more nerve than he did! Not that he would tell her as much. At least, for once, he didn't have to feel so guilty about being the only cracker eating two meals a day. Then again, Phoebe wasn't a cracker. She was now getting a third meal, whereas Kit and the others wouldn't get to eat again until morning. Oh, well! That was out of his control.

"So, what was the fight about?" Finney asked.

"I'm zick and tired of beople making fun of mein accent, und I'm not koing to take it hanymore."

Finney could understand why people gave the girl a hard time about the way she spoke, even though he hadn't said a word about it. But since she brought it up, he had to ask. "Where are you from?"

"Germany."

"Germany? Never heard of it. Is that close to Dublin?"

Phoebe shook her head. "If it is, I'fe neffer peen to Duplin. Arh! I don't know."

Finney popped a few berries in his mouth. "Do your parents live on the plantation too?"

Phoebe shook her head again. "Nein, poth of zem died on zee foyage offer here."

Perhaps that had been the wrong question to ask. The last thing Finney wanted to do was upset Phoebe on their first planned sneak-out night. Both of her parents had died on the voyage? That had to be heartbreaking. He couldn't help but wonder if she had seen their bodies dragged past her and thrown to the monsters of the sea. But that wasn't the kind of question one can ask. He knew better. Maybe if he asked the right question, a non-offensive one, she would share more details. "So, your whole family was kidnapped and shipped off together?" he asked.

Phoebe swallowed a chunk of potato, "Nein, ve veren't kidnabed. Arh! Mein barents had poth peen harresded for not baying our taxes. Zey vere sdarffing nearly to death in brizon. Arh! Zey vere hoffered ein deal to come to zee colonies as hindendured zerffants for ein beriod of zeffen years. Zee deal vas, zat zey had to take me vith zem. Arh! Zey died, und I liffed. Zo now I'm sduck here peing ein slaffe until I'm twenty-one."

Finney probably should have felt sorry for Phoebe, with her losing both of her parents and all. But instead of pity, he was overcome with jealousy. If she were to be released at the age of twenty-one, she would have a whole lifetime of freedom ahead of her. Not him!

"Vat's wrong?" Phoebe asked.

Finney couldn't tell her. How self-centered would he sound to say he was thinking about his own freedom at a time when she was discussing the loss of her mother and father? It was bad enough to think that way. But to share it? No way. "Don't worry about it," he told her.

Phoebe wiped her mouth on her arm, "If I zaid zomezing zat hurt vu, I'd like to know vat it is. Arh! Vat did I zay?"

Finney shrugged. It's not that he wanted to keep his thoughts a secret forever. He would be happy to tell her, but not now. Now it was time to let Phoebe share her story. Darcy had always told him there is a time to listen and a time to talk and that if one would think before opening their mouth, they would know which time was which. This was definitely a time to listen.

"Out vith it halready!" Phoebe insisted.

Finney shook his head, choking back his tears. Phoebe wasn't going to let this go. He would have to tell her what he was thinking. And when he did, he wouldn't blame her if she never wanted to speak to him again. What kind of monster thinks about themselves right after their friend tells them about the tragic loss of their kin? Finney wished he had Kit's brain. If Kit were in his shoes, he'd have easily found a way to change the subject. But he wasn't Kit. "It's just, just," he stammered. "It's just that out of everybody I've met here, I'm the only one who has no hope of freedom."

"Of courze vu haffe hobe. How long is your term?"

That went over better than Finney had thought it would. If Phoebe was hurt or upset with him, she didn't show it. "The rest of my life," he said. "I didn't come as an indentured servant. A group of rogues raided my home, and snatched me and my brothers and sisters right out of our living room."

"Zat is terriple!" Phoebe said. "Zey cannot get avay vith zat!"

"That's what I thought too, at least when it first happened," Finney said. "Poor folks in Dublin kept disappearing off the streets and people were saying slave traders were working the area. My uncle, Keir, I hadn't seen him for quite some time. A friend of my family told me Uncle Keir had gone out trying to stop the slave traders from taking anyone else from our area. With my whole heart I believed he was going to rescue me. But that was before I got on the ship and came to the colonies."

"I'm zo zorry to hear zat, Finney. Put don't giffe up hobe. Maype your uncle vill sdill find ein way to come und rescue vu."

"I have reason to believe that's not going to happen."

"Vu do? Vat makes vu zink that?"

Knowing how much or how little to tell was difficult. Phoebe seemed trustworthy, but what if he was wrong about her? What if she went back to the smoked Irish cabin and told the others of his thoughts and concerns about the planter? Perhaps this was a time to follow Darcy's advice. She had often told him that the only way to find out if a dog is trustworthy is to leave meat on the table.

"Phoebe, I'm trusting you to keep everything I tell you a secret. I don't want anybody else to know what we're talking about tonight. Now I know how ridiculous this sounds, but I think Master Levi Stone is not the planter's real name. I believe Master Levi is Uncle Keir in disguise."

"Vu're right. Zat does zound riticulous. Vy vould your uncle, ein man fighding for beople's freedom, come to zee colonies and ovn slaffes? Zat doesn't make any zenze."

"I know it doesn't," Finney said. "I can't understand it myself. If he's really my uncle, he should have noticed the resemblance when he saw me on the auction block. Surely he wouldn't have bid on me, knowing I might disclose his true identity. But he looks, sounds, and carries himself just like my uncle. I've even asked myself if maybe uncle Keir had a twin nobody ever told me about or something."

For a moment Phoebe stared deep into Finney's eyes as if she were trying to determine whether or not he was being serious. She didn't say a word; neither did he. What Finney expected Phoebe to say, he didn't know. But he sure hoped she would say something soon.

"Maype," Phoebe grinned, "Master Leffi Sdone really is your Uncle Keir, und he's only bretending to pe ein fierce slaffe ovner. Maype he has ein blan to puy slaffes as he can afford zem, und zen zecretly free zem und get zem pack to zeir ovn beople?"

"You're making fun of me, aren't you?" Finney asked.

"Nein. Not at all. It's zomezing ve could dream of anyvay, right?"

"If he were only pretending to be a wicked slave owner, he wouldn't have branded me and allowed the mulattos to whip and make fun of me the way he did, when he knows I'm his nephew."

CHAPTER ELEVEN

STORM OF STORMS

Normally, Finney loved storms but this one was downright frightening. A loud clap of thunder rattled the walls, and lightning illuminated the cracks around the door. The wind was howling terribly. An enormous crash and a series of horrific screams infiltrated the cabin. Finney didn't know what happened, nor was he sure he wanted to know.

"What was that?" Henry asked frantically.

"I don't know," Newt told him. "But I'll check it out. Stay in here with your mother."

Finney was torn. Half of him wanted to accompany Newt outside. The other half had no desire to leave the safety net of their cabin. Practically frozen in fear, he squeezed his eyes shut and gritted his teeth. He covered his ears, but it did nothing to block out the sound of loud, panicked voices both inside and outside of their shack.

"Be careful," Cherish said in a loud, concerned whisper.

As Newt opened the door, Finney's eyes popped open. A low, close lightning bolt shot down. It was so close, Finney thought it hit Newt. He wondered how long this storm might last. Surely it was almost over!

The wind whisked the door out of Newt's hand. Newt grabbed it with both hands and struggled against the wind to get it closed as he braved the storm. Finney wasn't sure he wanted Newt to go out there. What if he got struck by lightning? Or something worse happened to him? People were already out there screaming. Why should somebody else put their life on the line?

Cherish held Henry tight in her arms and gently rocked him back and forth. Finney wished he had someone to snuggle up to. He hugged himself tightly, eyes as wide as quarters.

"I don't like this," Harriet said.

"None of us do," Cherish replied. "But it'll be okay. God knows what He's doing. He can control where that wind blows, and how hard. He can control how low that lightning strikes, and whether or not it hits anything. God decides how fast that rain falls, and whether or not any flooding will occur. Everything will go just as He has it—"

William jumped out of his bed and onto his feet, "That does it! Do none of you people realize it's time to sleep? So, what if there's a little thunderstorm going on outside! In the morning we're gonna—"

The door burst open, and half of the slaves in the cabin either gasped or jumped, or both.

"Didn't mean to startle you," Newt said, wrestling the door closed behind him. "The wind took it right out of my hand again. A tree fell on the smoked Irish cabin. That's what all of the commotion is about."

Finney hugged his knees. If a tree fell on the other cabin, what was to stop one from falling on his? Especially if God was real, and didn't approve of Finney stealing that food. Then again, if Kit were right, God probably wouldn't punish him anyway. Why would God care what the devil's child did?

"Did anybody get hurt?" Cherish asked.

"No serious injuries, not as far as I could tell anyway," Newt told her. "There might be a few cuts and bruises, but other than that I think everybody's good."

"Oh, what a relief!" William said sarcastically. "Listen! All of this worrying and grumbling over what's going on at the smoked Irish cabin isn't going to help anybody. We're gonna have a lot of work to do tomorrow. We need some sleep. Let me say this as politely as I know how. Can everybody please—"

Another crack of thunder rattled the walls.

Henry, and a couple of other children in the cabin started crying. A knot swelled up in Finney's throat, but he refused to give in. He was too old to cry over something as piddly as a storm.

"Should we invite the smoked Irish and mulattos to cram in here with us until things calm down out there?" Cherish asked.

What a terrible idea! If those mulattos came into the white nigger cabin, they'd force all of the crackers out of their beds so the smoked Irish wouldn't have to sleep on the floor. They might even lock all of the crackers outside and make them endure the storm without shelter.

Harriet spoke before Finney worked up the nerve to do so, "There's not enough room in here for that many people. Not even temporarily."

"I'm not saying they could fit in here comfortably," Cherish said. "There's no doubt it would be a tight fit, but we could probably cram everybody in here somehow if we need to."

Finney wished that woman would close her mouth before others. The last thing he wanted was others to start feeling the same way she did. It was bad enough having to work for those mulattos during the day. Spending the night with them would be horrific. The smoked Irish, on the other hand, Finney wouldn't have a problem with. It did bother him that they were treated better than the white crackers were. But Phoebe and the other smoked Irish would likely come in, lay down somewhere, and go to sleep without causing any strife.

"The smoked Irish cabin is not our problem!" William barked. "We have to take care of ourselves. Now let's all settle down and go back to sleep."

"We can't do that," Kit protested. "The other cabin probably has rain pouring in. If things were the other way around, they would help us."

William glared at him. "Are you out of your mind? Do you really believe those mulattos or even the smoked Irish would lift a finger to help us? I don't care if this place was burning to the ground. They don't care about anybody but themselves, and quite frankly, neither should we."

"It doesn't matter," Harriet said hatefully. "I tell you, it doesn't matter one bit how anybody else would treat us. We have to do what's right, and all of us know what that is!"

Newt raised his hand and motioned for everyone to keep calm. "I don't think we'll have any say-so in that," he said. "Master Levi's out there surveying the damages now, and it'll be up to him if and how we respond."

William stomped his feet a couple of times and jumped in the air. Flailing his one arm, he yelled, "What is wrong with you people? This is a simple matter. Go... to... sleep. If we need to get involved, Master Levi or one of the mulattos will let us know. Now let's stop all of this back-and-forth rambling, close our eyes, shut our mouths, and get some rest so we can get up on time in the morning!"

As immature as William was being, his tantrum appeared to work. Now Finney understood why Kit was always worried about waking him. For the first time in a while, the cabin was silent. But the silence didn't last long. Somebody was either mumbling or whispering something. Finney strained his ears to listen. Soon, he recognized the voice. It was Kit, and he was praying. "I don't understand why You let people get hurt or why You let their cabin get tore up. But I know You must have a reason."

Finney shook his head. That lad was either brave or downright crazy. If William heard him, a war was going to break out! Still, in a way, he was jealous. Henry was being loved on by his mother. Kit was talking to his *Father*. The only way Finney could follow suit, he supposed, was to talk to the devil. Somehow that didn't seem appropriate. The last thing the lad wanted to do was give God a reason to aim one of those lightning bolts right at his head!

The harder it rained outside, the louder Kit prayed, "Help me be more like Paul. I don't want to let circumstances get me down. I don't want to always be suspicious of people. But it's hard. You know what I'm talking about, God. I probably shouldn't even say it out loud. But I still can't get over the planter taking that long trip and coming back with William. Something about that isn't right. I know it's none of my business, but God, somehow would you let me know what's going on? Where does Master Levi keep going when he leaves this place for so long?"

Duncan burst through the door, interrupting the prayer. In that slow, eerie-sounding voice of his, he said, "Everybody get your clothes on, and head outside."

As much as he didn't want to, Finney leaped out of bed, threw his breeches on, and joined the others in rushing outside. Between the darkness and the heavy rainfall, it was hard to see more than a few feet in front of him. Several quick flashes of lightning gave Finney a chance to see the vast number of tree limbs and debris strewn everywhere, and the smoked Irish shack that was now in ruins.

"The creek's rising!" Master Levi shouted over the roar of the wind and water. "Get whatever you can find and build a wall right here," he ordered, drawing a long line with his hand. "We've got to do everything we can to save the buildings!"

Smoked Irish, crackers, and mulattos ran every which direction as Master Levi barked commands.

Finney rushed toward the barn, searching for anything he could use to add to the wall. On his way, he plowed into Phoebe so hard they both fell down. "I'm so sorry," he told her. "Here, let me help you up," he said, rising to his feet and extending a hand down to her.

"Ah! Aren't vu sveet?" Phoebe said, taking Finney's hand and allowing him to lift her off of the soaked ground.

"I'm glad you didn't get hurt when the tree fell on your cabin," Finney said.

"Me too. One of zee tree limps came right through zee roof. I'm amased it didn't hit hanypody."

"Maybe I shouldn't say it," Finney chuckled, "but there's a few mulattos it could have hit, and I wouldn't have complained too much."

"Me neizer! I hate haffing to schare ein capin vith zem. Achan is zee vorst py far. Zen akain, I'm zankful I'm not in your capin eizer. Vu schould hear zee vay zoze guys talk about zee vite niggers. Oh, I did it akain. I'm zorry. How zey talk apout zee vite slaffes, I mean. It's terriple."

Finney looked around, knowing he and Phoebe could both get in serious trouble for having such a conversation, especially at a time when they were supposed to be working to save the plantation. But he had to know what she was talking about. "What do they say about us?"

"Terriple, terriple zings. Zomehow, zey zink it's funny veneffer one of vu gets ein vibing. Zey combete to zee vo can peat zee most vides effery day. Zey do hefferzying zey can to get Masder Leffi to zink zee vite niggers are

85

trouplemakers zo he'll pe harter on zem. Zey're zee reazon vu all only get one meal per day. If Achan had his vay, vu'd brobably only get to eat one meal effery ozer day. Lisden, I'fe brobably halready zaid more zan I schould haffe. Ve schould get pack to vork pefore hanzypody zees us."

The thunder rattled the ground so hard, Finney's entire body trembled.

"I agree," he told her. It was nice talking to you again."

CHAPTER TWELVE

TRAGEDY STRIKES

Just after daybreak, Cherish shouted in a frightened, yet angry voice, "Henry! Where are you?"

It was the third time she had yelled his name in the last minute. Still, there was no answer. She was walking faster than Finney had ever seen her walk before. "Where is that boy?" she grumbled, looking around frantically.

Newt, Finney, Kit, and Harriet were all looking for the lad as well. Finney wasn't about to say it out loud, he was beginning to think either Duncan or Cuddy had done something to him. Neither of them were in sight. He sure hoped the lad hadn't done something wrong. Surely he was too small to be getting hitched up to the whipping post.

"No! No!" Newt suddenly hollered from a distance. "No!"

"Did you find him?" Cherish screamed, running toward her husband's cries.

Newt didn't have to answer. Like Cherish, Finney was confident Newt had found their little lad. From the sounds of it, he could only assume Duncan and Cuddy were about to give Henry a beating. As much as he didn't want to see or hear it, he ran along behind Cherish.

Within seconds, Newt climbed up out of a creek bank, cradling Henry's lifeless body in his arms. The man was sobbing louder than Finney had ever heard a man sob. Newt fell to his knees and laid Henry on the ground. Cherish kept running, tears now streaming down her face.

Finney stopped running. He was too afraid to see Henry close-up. From all appearances, the lad was dead. He certainly hoped that wasn't the case. But if it was, he didn't want to see him.

Newt leaned over Henry. "No! No!" he continued hollering. "No!"

Cherish pushed her husband out of the way, cautiously touched the lad's forehead, and screamed, "My baby!" She grabbed his shoulders and gently shook him. "Henry! Henry! Come back to me now!" The lad didn't move.

Cherish slid her arms under the little one and scooped him up. Finney caught a better look at him. Henry's whole body was a bluish-purple color. "My baby! My baby!" Cherish screamed. "Why did it have to be my baby?"

Newt looked up at the sky for a moment before running across the field at full speed. Finney didn't watch to see where he went. Instead he kept his focus on Cherish and Henry. Oh, how he wanted to see that boy move, if even for a second. To see some kind of life come back into him.

"Please, Henry! Don't leave me! Please, baby! Please come back to your momma!"

For a second, it looked like Henry's hand moved. Finney watched closer. Surely he wasn't dead. He couldn't be.

"Henry! Henry! Come back to me! Please!" Cherish continued screaming as tears poured down her face. "Somebody, help my baby! Please! Somebody, do something!"

No. Apparently seeing the lad's hand move was nothing more than wishful thinking. Finney wished there was a way to ignore Cherish's hysterical crying. He wasn't the only one. For once, nobody was talking. Nobody was working. Nobody was doing anything but watching Cherish and her little one.

If somebody were to blame, and someone always was, it was God. From what Finney had gathered, God was in charge of everything. He could have stopped that rain or kept Henry out of the creek. God could have done something to save that little lad, but He didn't. Why? What kind of God would allow a little lad to die while his parents were working so hard to save their master's property?

And there knelt Kit, praying to the party responsible not only for allowing him to get his feet burned to a crisp but who created the very storm that caused Henry's possible death. What was wrong with him? Finney felt like trying to knock some sense into his hard head but doubted it would do any good. By now, he had been around enough believers to know he couldn't easily sway one's mind.

Out of nowhere, a pain-filled shriek filled the air. The voice was undeniably clear – it belonged to Newt. He screamed a second time. Cherish hugged Henry's lifeless body even tighter, closing her eyes.

Finney and most of the other slaves rushed toward the horrifying screams. Newt was strung up to the whipping post, every bit as naked as Finney had been for his welcome-to-the-plantation beating. Achan was tearing his flesh with the whip.

Had he not been terrified of being tied to that post again himself, Finney would have demanded the mulatto leave Newt be. Seeing a man beaten to a bloody pulp less than minutes after discovering his son had quite likely died was infuriating, especially when Finney knew there was no chance Newt had done anything to deserve such treatment.

Duncan and Cuddy were cheering Achan on, "That white nigger ain't been whooped for a long time!" Duncan hollered.

"That's right," Cuddy joined in. "He's far overdue. Make sure you get him good!"

Newt screamed out in agony as the whip tore into him again. Finney nearly hurled. He couldn't stand watching the man be beaten, knowing how much anguish he had to be in.

Hearing what sounded like a faint giggle, Finney turned around. Jane whispered, "What are you looking at me like that for? Newt's the one who was murmuring about Master Levi."

Finney remembered Harriet's words; she said everything that came out of Jane's mouth was a lie. He was starting to think she was right. Newt wasn't one to badmouth anybody. But even if he had, he just lost his little boy. That would be enough to cause anybody to do things they wouldn't normally do.

"Did Master Levi hear Newt speaking poorly of him?"

"Not word for word. He overheard Newt and I having a debate; he asked what was going on, and I told him. I was simply reminding Newt that on this plantation, complaining about Master Levi or the mulattos is strictly forbidden."

"Ayyyy!" Newt cried out before Finney had a chance to respond. "Ohhhh... Ah! Ah! Ah! Ohhh!"

Finney couldn't take it anymore. "Stop it!" he hollered. "I demand you stop right now!"

Achan turned and glared at Finney, "You talkin' to me that way, white nigger?"

For once, Finney wasn't scared. Whether Jane was telling the truth or lying like she normally did made no difference. Those brutes had to take Newt off that post. He needed to be with his family, not tormented by a bunch of ruthless tyrants. "I'm not a white nigger, but yes, I am talking to you. Leave that man alone!"

"You want me to quit tearing this white nigger's flesh?" Achan laughed. "Because you're tellin' me to?"

Finney said, "Because it's the right thing to do!"

"The only way he's getting off this post is when I decide enough lashings have been given out. Either to him or to one of you. Anybody wanna take his place?"

Finney's courage suddenly left him. As much as he knew he should probably volunteer to stand in for Newt after everything Newt and Cherish had done for him, he couldn't bring himself to do it. The thoughts of that whip cutting into him again was more than he could bear.

Kit piped up from a few feet behind Finney, "I'll take his place," he yelled.

Why was Finney not surprised that of everybody standing there, it would be Kit who would speak up? Sometimes the lad wished he could understand Kit's thought processes.

The mulatto laughed, "You'll take his whipping?"

Kit didn't bat an eye, "Yes, sir."

How could Kit say yes without a second of hesitation? He had to have known Achan would take him up on the offer. Finney cringed. He couldn't stand the thought of watching Newt take any more lashes, nor the thought of Kit, still sore from all he'd gone through, getting whipped on. But he'd already spoken up, and nobody had listened. Unless he volunteered to be the stand-in, Kit was setting himself up for a beating.

"Let me make sure you understand," Achan said. "If you take his place, I'm not going to go easy on you just because those burned feet make it difficult for you to walk. You'll take a man-size whipping, not a lad-size one. Got me?"

Kit crawled toward the whipping post on his hands and knees. As he got closer, he stopped and took his shirt off. "There's always hope," Phoebe's words replayed in Finney's mind. Maybe, just maybe something would happen and Achan would release Newt and not whip Kit. Was that too much to hope for?

"Get your breeches off, and hobble on up here if you're serious," Achan laughed.

Oh, what was the point of hoping? Kit stared Achan in the eye as he took off his breeches. Once his clothes were on the ground, the lad forced himself to stand. Finney's entire body went numb. How could Kit put himself in such a humiliating position, knowing what was to come, yet stand there looking so bold and confident.

"I'm ready whenever you are," Kit said.

Achan laughed, "Alright, cracker. Give me a second, and we'll swap you out for the big fellow."

Duncan and Cuddy gave Achan a look Finney perceived as one of disapproval. With less enthusiasm than normal, they took Newt off the whipping post. "You got lucky this time," Duncan told him. "You better hope there's not a next time, or your luck will run out."

Achan motioned for Kit to make his way to the post. "You're going to regret this," he said, with a slight snicker.

Nothing was funny about whipping a lad who could barely even stand. Those mulattos made Finney sick.

Kit kept a straight face as Duncan and Cuddy tied him to the post.

"Newt, you're to watch every lash. No turning your head. No closing your eyes. You're the reason this lad is getting the whip. You think about that every time he gets cut."

Newt's tears and trembling body spoke the words his mouth was unable to utter.

"The same rules apply for the rest of you. You came to see what's going on, so you will witness every bit of this foolish cracker's punishment. Anybody who walks off, looks away, or closes their eyes will be volunteering for the next thrashing," Achan warned before walking over to look Kit in the eye. "Are you ready for your man-sized whipping now?"

Kit's whole body tensed. "Yes, sir. I'm ready," he said.

Finney's heart beat every bit as fast as it would have had he been the one on that post. His breathing shallowed. Oh, if there was only something he could do to stop this! Something that didn't involve getting himself bloodied.

Achan stepped back into place, looked at Newt and said, "This is your doing," just before swinging that whip full force, and cutting the center of Kit's back.

Kit let out a loud hiss. Oh, how Finney wished he hadn't come to see what that loud shriek had been about. He wanted no part of this. But there was no choice.

The whip cracked again. As another line of blood appeared on Kit's lower back, the lad let out a horrific scream. Finney tried to think about something else. Anything else. But he couldn't ignore the horrific abuse unfolding before his very eyes.

CHAPTER THIRTEEN

CAMPING OUT

That Master Levi was nothing more than an overgrown bully! Why else would he force the white crackers to give up their cabin and sleep outside until the new cabins for the smoked Irish were built. And why, after the building project, would each colored family get their own shack, when all of the crackers would still have to bunk together? From what Phoebe had told him, the mulattos were a big part of the reason Master Levi treated the crackers worse than all of the others. He was just glad he wasn't amongst those assigned to work on the new huts. He'd rather stay out in the fields any day than to build homes he would never be allowed to step foot inside of.

Gazing at the stars helped Finney free his mind from Master Levi and his unfair practices. How did those stars get up there in the first place? And what kept them from falling? That's what he wanted to know. Well, that, and if anybody in Dublin was looking up and seeing the same stars he was.

"You're still awake too, aren't you?" Kit whispered.

"I am," Finney replied, temporarily forgetting the two were no longer friends. "Too much on my mind to fall asleep, I suppose."

Kit giggled, "I bet I know what you're thinking about. Or maybe I should say *who* you're thinking about."

Finney quickly remembered his earlier spat with Kit, but if Kit was ready to put it behind them, so was he. "I don't know what *or who* you're talking about," he said. "Unless you mean Henry and Cherish."

"Henry and Cherish? Really?" Kit asked. "Okay, let's go with that for a minute. What was going through your mind."

"Nothing just now. But earlier I kept picturing Cherish's face when she was crying over her baby. Henry was such a sweet kid. And his momma seems like the best one I've ever met. I don't know. I hate seeing people cry. And I hate it when people have to say goodbye. I don't reckon I've ever been around somebody who has died so young."

"Me either," Kit said. "My heart breaks more for Cherish than it does for Henry though. I know he's in a better place now. That lad's blessed. He went through his whole life without ever having Master Levi or any of the mulattos take a whip to him. That's more than the rest of us can say. Now for Cherish, I have no idea how she must feel. But all of her weeping made me cry right along with her. That's for sure."

For a brief time, neither of the lads spoke. Even though they hadn't known each other long, Finney saw

Henry like another little brother. He was going to miss the funny little man. He'd especially never forget the day when he asked who Miss Chiff was and why anybody would fall into her. If life after death truly existed, whoever was around that little one should consider themselves quite fortunate.

"Now that we've been serious for a minute and talked about a tragedy," Kit said, "what do you say we lighten the mood a little before we go to sleep?"

"Sure," Finney agreed. "Do you want to talk about those star patterns?"

"No," Kit said. "I want to talk about who you were thinking about right before we started talking about Cherish and Henry."

"What do you mean?"

"You know who I'm talking about," Kit insisted. "Phoebe. You like her, don't you?"

Finney shook his head. How did Kit know anything about his new acquaintance? It didn't matter. They were friends. Nothing more, nothing less. "You know it's not right for a smoked Irish and a cracker to like each other," he whispered.

"Says who?"

"Says... says... everybody."

Kit chuckled, "Since when does what *everybody* says make something right? You know you have a crush on Phoebe, Finney. You might as well admit it."

Finney shook his head, "I do not have a crush on Phoebe. Or on anyone else for that matter."

"Okay," Kit said, "And I guess dogs don't wag their tails either, huh?"

Suddenly Kit stopped talking and gave a head nod, hinting for Finney to turn and look behind him. There, towering over him was William. "Do you lads really think I'm going to stay awake two nights in a row? You don't want to see me angry."

He was right about that. Finney had a feeling what he'd seen the night before was nothing compared to what that man was capable of. He shook his head. "Sorry, sir."

"Oh, don't try none of that 'sir' stuff with me. I know what you're doing. You're trying to get on my good side so I'll overlook your girly little giggling over here. It's not going to happen."

"We're sorry, William," Kit said softly. "We'll let you go back to sleep."

"Oh, I'm going back to sleep alright! But it's not because you're *letting* me. It's because the two of you are gonna scoot your behinds over there!" William pointed to an area off in the distance where none of the other slaves were, "Way over there! And if you want to live until tomorrow, I would highly suggest you make the move now."

Kit scrambled to his feet, and Finney followed suit.

With his arm still extended in the direction he wanted them to go, William snapped his fingers, "Scoot!"

Kit smiled. "Come on, Finney. If we're over there by ourselves, we can talk all night if we want to. Thanks for the idea, William."

That Kit! He could find the positive in everything! Finney only wished he could be more like him.

With his feet still tender, Kit had to move slowly, but Finney was thankful he could at least use his feet again.

The boys walked quietly passed all of the other slaves, hoping not to wake anybody else.

Once the lads arrived at their new, more private sleeping space, Kit chuckled, "Still thinking about her?"

"About who?" Finney muffled a laugh.

"I thought so."

Finney wouldn't have been thinking about her had Kit not kept bringing her up. But since he had, the lad had to figure out his feelings. Was Kit right? Was he sweet on Phoebe? She was a nice girl, and a pretty one too. But she was a smoked Irish and he was a cracker. Not only that, but she was older than him. Guys were supposed to be the older ones in relationships, not girls. Phoebe wasn't like any of the other girls Finney had ever met, though. She was brave and strong, courageous even. Maybe Finney did like Phoebe, even if his family wouldn't approve.

"You didn't deny it," Kit said after a moment of silence.

Finney grinned. "Okay," he said. "I'll admit it. I am thinking about Phoebe. Now that I've admitted it, you have to tell me who you're thinking about."

Kit giggled again, "I'm not thinking of anybody. I just couldn't sleep because of how cold it is out here."

Finney hadn't given the temperature much thought. He turned his head to look at Kit. The lad was shivering. Remembering how Kit helped him on his first night at the plantation, Finney returned the favor. "Here," he said, pulling his shirt off. "Wrap this around you. It'll help a little."

"I can't take your shirt," Kit said. "You'll freeze."

"I insist," Finney replied. "I don't need it."

With that, Kit accepted the gift. "Thanks, Finney. I appreciate it."

Finney smiled. It felt good to do something kind for somebody else, especially when the deed wasn't likely to earn anybody a whipping, burning, or worse.

Kit sat up. "You know what this reminds me of?"

"What's that?"

"There was this prince that lived a long time ago named Jonathon. He befriended a shepherd by the name of David. They became such close friends that Jonathon took off his royal clothes and put them on David. It was a way for him to show David he didn't look down on him for not being a prince like he was."

Finney tried to picture a prince doing something like that, but every time he tried to picture one all he could see was Master Cyrus wearing a royal robe. Master Cyrus wouldn't have given up a royal garment for anybody!

"Where did you hear a story like that?" Finney asked.

"I heard about it at my old plantation. A lady there told me it came from the Bible."

"Of course," Finney muttered. "Where else would it have come from?"

CHAPTER FOURTEEN
CRAZY TALK

Finney didn't feel like talking to anybody, not after all that had taken place in the last twenty-four hours. This was one day when he wanted to work. So hard, in fact, that he would have no time to think about anything but his labor.

While most of the others were busy building the new slave shacks, Finney and Kit continued tending the fields. Per Master Levi's orders, the two lads had to put in an extra hour of work each day to make up for the labor lost due to those involved in the other project. That was okay by Finney as long as it meant he didn't have to help construct slave quarters he'd never be able to sleep in.

How he was chosen to be one of the two white crackers excused from the project, he didn't know. Although he did have to wonder if he was receiving special treatment of sorts because Master Levi really was Uncle Keir and had somehow figured out who Finney was. If that were the case, Finney's life on the Stone plantation might get a little easier.

In a way, that thought made Finney feel guilty, especially seeing as to how Kit had found the strength to do what he'd done. That whipping he took was far more brutal than the one Finney had received, and there he was, a few rows over, working himself nearly to death while whistling a joyous tune. Now and again, Finney would glance around and see the shirtless lad carefully pulling his breeches away from a wound. Finney didn't understand how he wore clothes at all. The breeches had to be preventing the cuts from scabbing over.

After a few hours of working in silence, Finney was finally ready to talk. "Sorry for not taking the whipping yesterday."

"There's nothing to be sorry about. I wanted to do it."

"Nobody wants to get whipped," Finney argued.

"I did."

If Kit wanted to get whipped, he either didn't feel pain or he was literally out of his mind. Finney continued working for a few minutes, while trying to view the situation from another angle. How was Kit seeing this whole thing? That somehow the other slaves would put him on a pedestal for doing the right thing? That what he did made him look strong and the others weak? That his bravery would somehow impress the mulattos and they would leave him alone in the future? No. There had to be something else. Oh, yes! That had to be it. "Let me guess, you wanted to because you're a believer, and the Bible tells you to, right?"

Kit chuckled sarcastically, "Promise not to turn this into a fight if I answer your question?"

"I don't feel like fighting about anything. You can talk about the Bible all you want to, and I won't insult you or your beliefs. You have my word on it."

Kit stopped working and crossed over into Finney's row. "This is probably going to sound incredibly stupid. But ever since I learned about Jesus, I've wondered how it would feel to take somebody else's punishment the way He did. And now I kinda know how He felt."

"What do you mean?" Finney asked.

"Exactly what I said."

"That doesn't tell me anything. I don't know anything about Jesus."

Kit smiled, "Okay. I'm sure we won't have much time for conversation, but I'll give you a quick summary now, and maybe we can talk more when everybody goes to sleep tonight."

"Sure," Finney said. "Sounds fair to me."

"Jesus is God's Son. For a while, He lived on earth just like you and me. But He never did anything wrong. He came to earth because people do things they shouldn't and could never do enough good things to get into Heaven. The Bible says the penalty for people's sin, or for doing things God says are wrong, is death. So Jesus, even though He hadn't done anything wrong, allowed men to whip him, kind of like I was whipped last night, in front of a big crowd of people. But they took it further and hanged him on a cross to die."

Why did Finney have to give his word? Not that he hadn't broken it before. Kit's "answer" was going to take forever! Perhaps things were better when they were working in silence. Looking up at the sky, he said, "It looks like it might start raining again. We should probably get back to work."

"You can start working if you want to, but I've got to tell you the rest of the story before I do. After Jesus died, they placed Him in a tomb. Three days later, He came back to life. Now He lives in Heaven with God the Father."

Finney continued working, as if he hadn't heard a word. Nobody dies and comes back to life. Sure, it would be nice to think living a second time was possible. Especially in situations like what happened on the Gillcrest plantation with Clement. If Clement could have come back to life after they hung him, that would have been amazing. But it never happened. And Phoebe's parents that died on their voyage, they didn't come back to life either. Maybe she had that hope though? If Finney were suddenly to find out his parents had died, he would like to think they could be raised from the dead and live again.

"You don't believe any of that, do you?" Kit asked when Finney didn't respond.

"I'm not sure what I think," Finney said. "But let's say I did believe it. If everything you said is true, if this Jesus died on a cross and then came back to life and somehow got back to Heaven, how does that make it possible for other people to get to Heaven?"

Kit laughed, "I guess I didn't explain that very well. To be guaranteed a home in Heaven, the Bible says all we have to do is believe everything I Just told you about Jesus and then pray and ask Him to save us."

"Right," Finney shook his head. "We just talk to somebody we can't see, ask him for a free ride to Heaven, and He says, 'Sure, here you go.' I'm sorry. I just don't believe that."

"You don't have to believe Master Levi or one of his mulattos would give you a whipping if you try to run, but that doesn't mean they won't do it."

Finney didn't want to argue, but at the same time he was tiring of the conversation. "Hey, I just felt a drop of water land on my arm. Let's get this field weeded."

Chapter Fifteen

TRUST BUILDING

Finney woke up to a hand over his lips. Opening his eyes, he saw Phoebe kneeling next to him, smiling. She motioned for him to follow her away from the others, who were still sleeping soundly.

Without hesitation, Finney quietly stood and followed her to the other side of the now destroyed smoked Irish quarters. "What are we doing?" he asked, once he was certain nobody was close enough to hear their conversation.

"I don't know. I vas chust out here looking for hansvers akain, und I kot lonely."

Finney laughed. "Oh, so I have to forfeit my sleep because you're lonely?"

"Isn't zat vat friends are for?"

Finney shrugged, "I reckon so."

"Finney, If I ask vu zomezing, do vu bromize to neffer tell hanypody I asked."

"I promise. What is it?"

"I'm zinking apout running avay, not only to get mein ovn freedom, put to sdart helbing ozer slaffes like us get zeirs. Vat do vu zink?"

Finney ran his fingers through his hair, remembering what he went through when he tried to flee the Gillcrest's place. He didn't wish that on anybody. At the same time, he didn't wish anyone to have to endure the hardships of slavery either.

"Vow. Vu're giffing zis ein lot of zought, aren't vu?"

"I don't know what to say. I ran away from my last plantation, and things went terribly wrong. My friend, Clement, got whipped and murdered for helping me escape. I got whipped worse than I ever had been before. Another man on the Gillcrest plantation had tried to run a couple of times before I did, and Master Gillcrest burned a huge letter "R" onto his cheek. Most of the people on that plantation wouldn't dare run because of what they'd experienced themselves or seen happen to others who had attempted it."

"Put vu're not most beople, are vu, Finney?"

"I'm not. You have no idea how often I think about trying to get free. About searching for my family. About trying to find my way home. I think about it all of the time. I wonder who might be able to help me or even escape with me. But then I think back to what happened to Clement and me, and ask myself if it's worth it."

"Is it?" Phoebe asked.

"If I was selfish, I would say yes! I'd ask you to run away with me. But I have to think about you too. See, I don't have any hope of being set free. You know you will be when you turn twenty-one. You can endure this until you're legally an adult, and then go out and have a normal life, or you can run away with me, possibly get caught, and if you're lucky just be beaten, and scarred up for the rest of your life. You'd be running from slave catchers, always looking over your shoulder, forever. If you're not so lucky, you could be crippled or killed for the offense. For you I don't know that it's worth it because you're already promised your freedom, and life will eventually get better for you."

"Zo vu zink mein pest obzion is sdaying here, und vu're pest obzion is running avay? Py yourself?"

Phoebe sounded upset. It sounded as though she were calling him a hypocrite. Or as though he somehow thought himself more capable of running away than she was. If only he could find the right way to give suggestions in such delicate situations! Perhaps it would be best not to acknowledge the first part of her question and only focus on the latter. "I don't know," he said. "That's why I'm still here. I have to make up my mind."

"It looks like I'm not zee only one vo is zearching for hansvers, huh? Let me ask vu hanozer gueszion. Vat vould vu zink of me if I decided to run away, rekardless of your zoughts on zee matder?"

Finney clasped his hands together over his head and took a deep breath. "I wouldn't think any more or any less of you," he said. "But I would certainly hope you'd take me with you."

"Vat? Und risk vu getting peaden or killed pecauze vu're helbing me?"

Phoebe's sarcasm told Finney he was right. She was upset. He doubted there was anything he could say or do to soften what had already been said. Again, he pretended not to recognize the harshness of her tone. "I would be willing to take the risk. And it wouldn't be only to help you. It would be for both of us."

Phoebe turned her back to the lad and slowly began walking away from him.

"Where are you going?" he asked.

"To look for hansvers. Vy don't vu do zee zame, und zen ve can talk about zis akain hanozer time?"

Ignoring Phoebe's frustration was not helping matters. As much as he didn't want to ask, Finney asked, "Are you mad at me?"

"Nein, nein, not at all. I chust don't zink zeze are decizions ve schould make in haste. Ve need to giffe hourzelffes time to make vadeffer decision zat vill pe pest for poth of us."

"Okay," Finney said with a sigh. "I'll spend some time thinking about it."

"Fery kood. Haffe ein kood night. Ve vill meet akain zoon."

"Good night," Finney said, before turning to walk back to the white nigger cabin.

The lad had no doubt it was going to be a long night. It sounded as though Phoebe already had her mind made up. She was going to make a break for it, with or without him. Deep down, Finney was determined to do the same. But for him, the knowing when, how, and with whom was the hard part. Somehow, he wanted to make a decision that night so he would be ready the next time he and Phoebe had a chance to speak.

Chapter Sixteen

CAN'T FOOL KIT

It wasn't very enjoyable to stare up at a cloud-filled night sky. Except for a small glimmer of moonlight in a clearing, everything was pitch black. Finney could only hope Kit wouldn't bring up what they'd talked about earlier.

No chance of that, though. "Are you ready to talk now, Finney?" he asked.

Finney closed his eyes, pretending to be asleep. He wasn't trying to be rude. He just didn't want to think about religious wives' tales. He'd rather lay there planning an escape in the event Master Levi Stone, or Uncle Keir, whoever the planter was didn't lighten his load.

"I know you're awake, Finney. Your light breathing is giving you away. We don't have to talk about it if you don't want to."

Not sure how to respond without hurting Kit's feelings or insulting him again, Finney tried to fake heavier breathing.

"Give it up, Finney," Kit said. "I get it. You'd rather talk about Phoebe, right?"

There went the whole idea of pretending to be asleep! Finney couldn't help but chuckle. "I'd rather not talk about anything right now. I just want time to think."

"I understand," Kit said. "You can better control your dreams about her when you're awake, right?"

Finney felt his face turning red. "Stop already. I'm not thinking about anybody in particular."

"Really? Even after that kiss you planted on her behind the outhouse yesterday?"

"What kiss are you talking about?"

Kit chuckled, "How many have there been?"

"None. What makes you think I kissed anybody?"

"Jane saw you."

"Of course! Everybody knows they can trust Lying Jane."

Kit laughed, "Lying Jane, huh? I haven't heard anybody call her that."

"Now you have," Finney said. "But I did not kiss Phoebe nor was I thinking about her. I was actually thinking about my future."

Kit chuckled sarcastically, "Your future? What could you possibly be thinking about your future? It's not like you're ever going to leave this place. You told me yourself that you're going to be a slave forever."

Finney shook his head. "No, I told you I was kidnapped and forced into slavery and that I don't have a contract limiting my stay to a certain period of time."

"What's the difference?"

"The difference, Kit," Finney said, getting angry, "is that Master Levi *thinks* I'm going to be his slave forever. Just because a person thinks something to be true doesn't mean it is."

"So, what? You think a magician is going to show up, say a bunch of gibberish while waving a rod in the air, and you'll be back in Dublin?"

"This conversation is over," Finney said.

"Why's that? Because you can't handle the truth?"

Finney stood, walked past all of the other white slaves, and bedded down alone. Finally, he could have some peace and quiet!

No, Finney wasn't expecting some odd spell-caster to show up! He didn't need them to. He could get off that plantation. He'd have succeeded before had he not relied on Clement to keep him safe for a night. The next time he escaped, Finney wouldn't count on anybody but himself.

That didn't mean he wouldn't accept help from another slave. For instance, if Phoebe wanted to run off with him or be a distraction so he could flee, Finney wouldn't tell her no. Now Kit, on the other hand, would be a different story altogether. He was too much of a do-gooder to be trusted with any scheming that might take place.

Finney closed his eyes and tried to drift off to sleep. But it was too late for that. He had already gotten his mind going ninety miles-per-hour. After what happened to Clement, how could the lad even consider allowing somebody else to get involved? He wouldn't be able to live with himself if anybody else got whipped or burned or killed because of him.

Still, that wouldn't stop him from daring an escape on his own.

Somebody's footsteps were getting close. Finney was certain he knew who they belonged to but looked up nonetheless. "Why did you follow me?" he whispered.

"To apologize," Kit said. "I didn't behave very Christian-like back there. I shouldn't have made fun of you. The more I thought about it, the more I realized what you meant about not being a slave forever. You're thinking about running, aren't you?"

"No," Finney lied. "I wouldn't consider doing such a thing. All I meant is a person never knows what might happen in life. Something deep inside tells me I won't spend the rest of my days as a slave. I don't know how my freedom will come about. But it will."

"Finney, I hear your words, but to be honest, I feel like you're leaning toward taking off. Please don't. If you do, a lot of people will get hurt."

"Like who?"

"Did you see Cherish on your way over here?"

"For a second," Finney admitted. "But I turned my head. I couldn't bear to watch her."

"Let's talk about what you couldn't bear to watch, Finney. That woman was cradling a bundle of Henry's clothing as if it were him. She was rocking those clothes back and forth and crying, 'My baby. My poor, sweet, innocent baby.' Finney, I saw her lean over and kiss those clothes as if she were kissing Henry's cheek. She's falling apart."

"I know, alright?" Finney said. "Cherish is hurting every bit as badly as any parent who loses their child. But what does that have to do with me leaving this place?"

"If you run away, that woman is going to hurt even more. She's going to see it that another child has disappeared. And if they catch you, and you get killed. Oh, Finney. She's going to lose her mind for good. Do you really want to be responsible for that?"

Finney shook his head, "I don't even know why we're having this conversation. I already told you; I'm not planning to run."

"You better not be," Kit said. "What you ought to be doing right now is helping me be there for Cherish. Don't forget how she treated you the first day you met her. You remember that, right? We came into the cabin and you were laying there all bloodied up. She was the first person to go out of her way to clean you up and try to make you feel better. Now it's time for you to do the same for her. It's not a time to run out on a woman who did so much for you."

"I'm not you, and I'm not Cherish," Kit said. "I don't know how to help and comfort people. But I'm not going to run out and abandon anybody. Let's just drop it and get some sleep."

"Sure," Kit said. "Good night."

"Good night," Finney said, knowing it would be anything but. How could he sleep now that images of Cherish weeping over Henry and images of a whip crashing into him were circling around and around in his mind? Darcy always told him to think pleasant thoughts before going to sleep. She said it would give him better dreams. Oh, how he missed that lady! Yes, it would be much better to think about Darcy than to think about all of the horrors he had faced since arriving in the colonies.

CHAPTER SEVENTEEN

GONE

Master Levi Stone was fit to be tied. "Somebody had to have seen or heard something. Tell me what you know!" he demanded, pacing back and forth in front of the assembly of slaves.

All of the slaves – smoked Irish, cracker, and mulatto stood at full attention without speaking. Master Levi continued, "If, *or when*, I find out who's withholding information, that slave will receive a punishment far greater than any you have ever received or witnessed. I can't stand here all day. I've got a slave to catch. Achan, Duncan, Cuddy, get these slaves hopping, and don't let any of them out of your sight. Forget building the shacks today. Keep everybody weeding. If anybody else comes up missing, I'll hold the three of you accountable."

If Finney, or any of the other slaves, ever needed a motive to run, that last warning from Master Levi could certainly have given it to him. If he were to run, those three mulattos would pay the price, regardless of whether or not he was found. Finney wasn't sure if he was going to run just yet or not. But if he didn't, he sure hoped somebody else would follow Phoebe's lead.

Phoebe, Phoebe. The lad felt as though she had somehow pierced his chest and choked the life out of his tender heart. They were two peas in the same pod. How could she have deserted him like that? And why wouldn't she have at least said goodbye before running off?

As Master Levi headed toward the horse corral, Duncan growled, "You heard him. Get in that field, and work!"

Getting anything done during such a stressful time would be nearly impossible. But with Master Levi off the plantation, those mulattos were likely to go hog-wild in handing out discipline, especially to the white crackers. Regardless of how pained his mind was, Finney would force himself to persevere.

"Those under the age of twenty, *run* to the toolshed, load your arms with tools, and meet the group at the north field! I'll supervise the tool gatherers. Achan and Cuddy can accompany the rest. Let's go!"

Alongside several of his peers, Finney darted toward the toolshed. One of the smoked Irish female slaves tripped over nothing and landed flat on her face. Finney extended a hand to help her up.

"Nobody gave either of you permission to stop," Duncan scolded in a sluggish tone, "Get up, and follow orders, and you better be thankful I'm in a good mood."

Duncan was in a good mood? Somehow his scowl had given Finney the opposite impression. The lad wondered what it might be like to be a mulatto. To have so much power and control over the other slaves? He also wondered how stupid one must be to fulfill such duties while Master Levi was away? If Finney were a mulatto, he'd have set everybody free the second Master Levi left the property. The planter would return to find an empty plantation.

In no time, the younger slaves caught up to the older ones just as they were entering the north field. Cuddy, who had been accompanying the adults, stared at Finney with a sinister grin. Finney hated that look. He'd seen it too many times not to recognize it.

"White nigger!" Cuddy called. "Drop those tools, and get over here."

Not wanting trouble, Finney complied with a softspoken, "Yes, sir."

"Remember me, white nigger? I'm one of the men who strapped you to the whipping post that day you got here, and then had the privilege of watching your face as you were taught who rules this plantation."

Was Finney supposed to be impressed? The man continued, "I wish you could have seen what I did. Your face was filled with hatred, embarrassment, and pure terror – and that was before the whip ever touched you. You haven't forgotten that day, have you, cracker?"

Finney shook his head, "No, sir." Oh, how he hated that evil man! No, he hadn't been the one who had branded him, nor the one who had whipped him. But he had mocked his agony and humiliation in a way that no decent human being would have.

Playfully holding up his whip, Cuddy said, "You sure you haven't forgotten? I'd be happy to give you a reminder if you need one."

Smelling danger, Finney was cautious with his reply, "I remember it well, sir. It taught me better than to ever rebel against you, the other mulattos, or Master Levi. I won't ever give you any trouble."

Cuddy's smile grew wider. "You know anything about that runaway slave?"

That was his angle! Cuddy was going to use Phoebe as his excuse to torment him.

"No, sir," the lad said. "I didn't know she was gone until this morning when Master Levi told everybody."

"Are you sure about that? My daughter said you and Phoebe recently shared some alone time together."

Finney wondered how the man's daughter, whoever she might be, knew anything about that. Perhaps she was friends with Phoebe? Either that or she was some kind of spy. But who was she? That Finney would need to figure out right quick!

"Was my daughter right?"

Finney could tell Cuddy already knew he had been alone with Phoebe. There was no point in lying about that. Attempting to cast doubt on the integrity of the whip-bearer's child would be a foolish move anyway. "Yes, sir," Finney said. "I spent time with her, but she didn't say anything about running away."

"So, you have no idea where she is or when she took off?"

"No, sir."

"You better hope that's true. I'm gonna keep my eye on you, cracker. You get to work and don't even think about slacking off or talking to anybody."

Chapter Eighteen

BROKEN

Another tear leaked out of Finney's eye as he lay, wishing more than anything, to fall asleep, never to wake again. Holding his belly, he rolled onto his left side. It wasn't fair. Phoebe lied. She said running away wasn't a decision that should be hastily. That they should both think on it so they could discuss it the next time they saw each other. Some friend she turned out to be!

Finney squeezed his eyelids together as tightly as possible, even though he knew it wouldn't do him any good. Phoebe was going to get caught, just like he had been. Master Levi Stone was much rougher than the Gillcrests ever thought of being. At least she wasn't a white cracker. That might make them go a little easier on her. Oh, why should he care what they did to her? She left without saying a word. That girl wasn't concerned about anybody but herself. Perhaps Finney would be better off thinking the same way.

"Stop sniffling, or go outside!" William snapped.

Finney hadn't even realized he'd been sniffling. But all of that crying made his nose run. What was he supposed to do? Let his nasal fluids run down his lip? Flipping back onto his right side again, Finney mumbled, "I'm a nobody. Always have been. Always will be."

William jumped off his bed and onto the floor. Kit jumped up and stood in front of him. "Go back to bed, William. Finney and I'll go outside so you can get some sleep."

"I didn't say I'm going anywhere," Finney protested.

"Come on," Kit said. "You could use some fresh air, and a friend."

"Promise not to bring up prayer or God if I join you?"

Chuckling, Kit said, "Sure. I promise. But only this time."

"Five seconds," William said. "Both of you have five seconds to exit this cabin before I toss you out on your heads!"

Kit grabbed Finney's arm and jerked him out of bed. "Let's go before things get out of hand."

Finney didn't have enough mental strength left to put up a fight. Still crying, he hopped out of bed and accompanied Kit outside.

Kit wasted no time in lighting into him, "I can't believe you're this upset over Phoebe! You barely even know the girl!"

"Is that what you brought me out here for? To give me a hard time?"

"I brought you out here to keep William from bloodying your face. But since we're here, we might as well talk about this. Would you be this upset if I was the one who ran off?"

Finney didn't feel up to smiling, but his face did so anyway. What an awkward question!

"Seriously, Finney. I want to know. We've been friends a whole lot longer than you and Phoebe have been. Would you be acting like this if I were missing?"

"It's not just that she's missing," Finney said.

"Then what is it?"

"It's kind of hard to explain."

"Take your time, and figure it out. I've got all night!"

Finney slowly cracked his knuckles, one at a time. After the last one, he said, "Phoebe was different than pretty much anybody I've ever met. Almost every night, she would sneak outside and take long walks. She said she was looking for answers. Trying to figure out if there was a reason for all of life's difficulties. Even though I don't go about it the same way she does, I'm always trying to figure that out too."

Kit smiled, "I could help you understand it all, but I promised not to bring it up this time."

"Thanks for remembering," Finney said. "Somehow, I convinced myself Phoebe and I were going to be friends forever. I just don't understand why she would leave, and not even ask if I wanted to come with her."

"Haven't you been thinking of leaving, without asking me if I wanted to join you?"

Finney rubbed his hands together and looked Kit in the eye, "To be honest, yes. I have considered it."

"When you were thinking about leaving me here, did it ever cross your mind that I would be hurt? Or that I might lose sleep over you leaving? Or was your focus primarily on how you were going to pull it off without getting caught?"

That wasn't fair. Yes, Finney had thought about leaving. But he hadn't done it. He hadn't deserted anyone he cared about without having the decency to tell them goodbye. Of course, it was possible he could have done that in the future. But he hadn't. Without thinking about it, Finney stopped walking and glared at Kit. The lad had no right trying to make him look as selfish as Phoebe had been.

"You don't have to answer me," Kit said. "We both know Phoebe didn't do anything you wouldn't have done yourself."

"People like you are the reason my family despised believers," Finney retorted. "Christians always think they know everything about everybody. Thinking they're always right, and everybody else is always wrong. Judging people without any evidence."

"Speaking the truth is not judging you. As to whether or not I have evidence, the words that came out of your mouth just a moment ago provided all the evidence either of us needs. You admitted you had thought about leaving without asking me if I wanted to go with you. There's no difference between your thought process and Phoebe's."

"And how do you know what Phoebe was thinking? Did you ask her? Did she tell you? Let me guess. God told you, right?"

Tears streamed down Finney's face again. He didn't want to fight. He just wanted to understand how and why Phoebe left him like she did.

"I'm not trying to upset you, Finney," Kit said. "But to help you see things another way. If you know something I don't, then by all means, share it."

Finney dropped to his knees, crossed his arms on the ground in front of him, and buried his face in his arms. How could he have been so stupid? Why had he told Phoebe about how guilty he felt about what happened to Clement? That's why she left without telling him. She was afraid of getting him in trouble. But still, couldn't she have sent word by somebody else to tell him she was leaving?

Kit knelt down and placed a hand on Finney's shoulder. "It's going to be okay," he said. "You're not alone. You still have me."

Finney shook his head.

"What?" Kit asked.

"Are you saying you were better friends with Phoebe than you are with me?"

Talk about self-centered! What was Kit's problem? How many times was he going to compare the two friendships? This had nothing to do with him whatsoever!

Chapter Nineteen

FLASHBACKS

Finney didn't care how hard that rain was pouring on him, or that the mulattos wouldn't let him or any of the other slaves seek shelter. The place could flood all over again for all he cared. Phoebe was on the run. By now, slave catchers were probably hot on her trail.

The lad winced, suddenly feeling as though he were back in the woodshed at Clement's place, hearing an uproar of men he couldn't see and terrified as he heard the mob interrogating the Alloways. What a horrible night that had been! Another scene raced through his mind. A couple of men were ripping off Clement's shirt, while others were tying him to a tree. Master Josiah drew the whip back and swung that thing with what appeared to be every ounce of strength he had. The second it cut into Clement's back, Clement screamed in horrifying agony. Callum's heart was racing. He had to stop thinking about it. What happened on the Gillcrest plantation was in the past. It wasn't happening again. There was no reason to get so worked up over it.

"Break time's over, you filthy white nigger," Duncan's unhurried, spooky whisper came from just behind him. "There's no time for idleness. Get back to work!"

"Yes, sir," Finney said, immediately grabbing and pulling out another weed, as the rain dripped from his hair onto the ground beneath him. He wasn't able to work long before a loud clap of thunder made him jump. In that instant, his mind took him back to Master Josiah ordering Ghazi and Jonah to peel his shirt off and attach him to the whipping post for running away. He remembered nervously fidgeting, closing his eyes, wishing with everything in him there was a way to avoid what he knew was coming. He remembered the terror of learning he had been turned over to Master Cyrus's authority and that it was his son who was going to be lashing him. He could hear that older teenager whispering in his ear, "You are mine, you poor-white earth scratching scum." Finney cringed. "I'm going to delight in your begging for mercy!" Oh, if there was only a way to shut off the memories! To get Master Cyrus's voice out of his head!

Duncan suddenly kicked him in the ribs, knocking him onto his side. With a sinister chuckle, he said, "What did I tell you, cracker? We're down a slave right now. There's no time for idleness! Get moving!"

"Yes, sir," Finney said. "I didn't mean to stop."

Duncan kicked him a second time. In that frighteningly stern, yet quiet and slow voice of his, he said, "You didn't mean to? Liar! You chose to stop working. Don't let it happen again!"

Finney wouldn't do it again. Not if he could help it anyway. Why couldn't he just continue on with life as the other slaves were? Everybody else was weeding those plants as if it was just a normal day. All of them had seen and experienced beatings before. Most of them had been around somebody who had run away. If they could all put that in their past, and move forward, so could he. And he did, for about ten minutes.

Without warning, his mind took him back to his first day on the Stone plantation. Cuddy and Duncan were holding his arms, while Achan yanked the breeches off of him. Mortified, the lad tried to cover himself, but Cuddy and Duncan held his arms so tight he couldn't move. They dragged him over to Master Levi Stone, who was holding a branding iron in the fire. Finney's lips began to quiver. His entire body tensed. Master Levi laid one end of the branding iron down in the fire, while grabbing the lad's right arm and turning him around. "I've got him," he said.

The mulattos released him, but Master Levi's firm grip wasn't going to allow him to go anywhere. With his other arm, Master Levi pulled the branding iron out of the fire and moved it toward him. Finney lurched forward just as the branding iron was about to be pressed against his backside.

A whip suddenly cut into his upper legs. Finney squalled in pain, falling face first into the dirt.

There came that hair-raising voice just above the sound of a whisper, "I'm starting to think you know something about the missing slave's whereabouts, cracker," Duncan said in an even slower, creepier manner than what was his normal. "Something sure has you distracted today."

"I don't know anything," Finney whined, holding the back of his legs, while looking back at Duncan through tear-clouded eyes.

"The truth always comes out. If you know where she is, you better speak up. The quicker you confess, the less severe your punishment will be."

Finney didn't want that whip to cut into him again, now or later. If he really thought a confession would make Duncan go easier on him, he would have made one up. But as far as he was concerned, the mulatto's words were nothing more than a manipulation tactic. If he confessed, Duncan would likely stripe him from shoulder to ankle again. If he didn't confess, and nobody else did either, he may end up in the same predicament. But at least that way, there was hope that somebody might step forward.

"I see you're thinking about it, cracker. Smart lad," Duncan whispered at the pace of a snail. "But I need an answer. Are you ready to speak up?"

Finney shook his head, "I don't have anything to confess."

"We'll see about that," Duncan said. "For now, get to weeding that field. If, I mean, when I find out what you had to do with that girl running off, you're going to wish you'd never met me."

Too late for that one! Finney already wished he'd never met the man, or anyone else in the colonies for that matter! Why couldn't he just go home, and find out this whole thing was a horrific nightmare?

Finney, for the next hour anyway, forced himself to work without having any more flashbacks. No one spoke to him, or to any of the other slaves, during that entire time period. But somehow, during those sixty minutes, several of the slaves ended up getting closer and closer to one another as they worked.

Eventually, Jane broke the silence, "I can't blame Phoebe for running off. Can you imagine how embarrassed she must be?

"About what?" William asked.

"You didn't hear about it? I'm not one to gossip, so I'm not going to tell everything I know, but that girl was flirting with a certain lad on this plantation," Jane paused. After glancing at Finney for a second, she continued, "She was sneaking off in the middle of the night to take long moonlit strolls with her new fellow. But get this. He wasn't a smoked Irish. He was one of our own."

"Where do you get this stuff?" Harriet interrupted. "We all live together. We would know if a lad in our cabin was sneaking out. William, you're a light sleeper. Have you seen anybody lurking about?"

"I sure haven't," William replied. "Has anybody else?"

All of the white slaves looked around in silence. Finney wasn't about to say a word. He wondered what else, if anything, Jane knew.

"You all think I'm lying, don't you?" Jane asked.

"I don't know," William replied. "But so far, I haven't heard anything that would have caused Phoebe to run away. Is there a point to this story?

Jane giggled, "Well, I hadn't gotten to the most interesting part. Phoebe found out that the cracker she was flirting with lied to her." She paused and glared at

Finney again. "You see, this cracker kept sneaking out and taking her *extra* food that he claimed he had stolen out of the main plantation house. You won't believe where it really came from! He was thieving food right out of her own cabin, and then feeding it to her. He convinced that girl he was doing her a favor, when he was actually helping himself to food that rightly belonged to her and the other smoked Irish!"

Finney felt horrible! How did Jane know all of that? She must have been spying on him. She undoubtedly told Phoebe everything just to see how she'd react! But he couldn't say so. Not now. Not in front of so many witnesses. He looked around the room in silence, pretending he had no idea what she was talking about.

"I don't believe a word of that," Harriet said.

"I'm with Harriet," William agreed. "Jane, you can say you're not a gossip all you want to, but you spread more rumors than anybody else on this entire plantation. And most all of them are rumors you started yourself."

Jane stopped pulling weeds and leaned toward William, "What happened, there, William? Did that bull steal your hearing when he stole your arm?"

"Now stop it, Jane!" Cherish scolded. "That kind of talk is completely unacceptable, and I, for one, will not tolerate it."

"What's all the fuss about?" Cuddy hollered, crossing the field.

"It's not really a fuss," Jane said. "William and Cherish were over here laughing about how funny they think it is that Phoebe was able to sneak right off of this plantation without Master Levi, you, or the other mulattos seeing her. They said you all must be pretty-"

"Now, Jane," Cherish interrupted. "You tell that man the truth. I won't settle for anything less."

"Me?" Jane laughed "Me, tell the truth? What other truth is there?"

No wonder Harriet and Phoebe had both fought with Lying Jane! She really was one mean-spirited girl. Finney wanted to say so. But those fresh cuts on his legs told him to keep his mouth closed. No matter what he said, Jane would dispute it, and when she did, Cuddy would side with her. The mulattos always did.

Cuddy examined the faces of all of the slaves occupying that section of ground. "Cherish, you come with me," he said after a minute or so of thinking on it. "The rest of you, spread out, get to work, and stop all that talking. William, if there's any more of that kind of talk, I will report it to Master Levi."

Finney rolled his eyes and hoped no one had seen him do so. With everything Cherish had already gone through, the idea of her getting whipped because of Jane's flat out lie made him sick to his stomach. Not only that, but he struggled to understand why, if Jane blamed both William and Cherish, Cherish was going to get whipped, but nothing was going to happen to William. Nor did he understand why if William violated Cuddy's order, why Cuddy wouldn't deal with him himself. Nothing made sense in the colonies, especially on the Stone plantation.

CHAPTER TWENTY

HARASSED

Two weeks had passed since Phoebe's disappearance, and Master Levi was anything but happy about it. "If you don't get any of these slaves to speak up and tell us what they know within the next seven days, there's going to be a change in authority," he threatened the mulattos. "I will demote every one of you and appoint three smoked Irish as your replacements. And you better believe every one of you will be severely whipped if you don't get answers soon."

What a terrifying yet exciting proclamation! Seeing the tables turned on those wicked brutes would be the highlight of Finney's time in the colonies. He'd love to hear their screams of horror as the smoked Irish lit into them. If he knew the mulattos as well as he thought he did, however, that wasn't going to happen. One way or another, they would get a confession out of somebody.

Master Levi continued his warning. "To be fair, for the next week, each of you mulattos will be given more authority than you've had in the past. You can do whatever it takes, short of burning or killing any of my slaves to get the truth out of them. Whoever aided in the escape or has knowledge of it must be brought to justice."

Finney glanced around.

Cuddy gave the lad a creepy grin. He swiftly grabbed the lad by the ear and led him away from the group. Letting him go, he stared him eyeball to eyeball, "I'm not going to lose my position here, cracker. Now you and I both know Phoebe told you about her plans. Now fess up, and don't spare any details."

Finney wondered what would happen if he sent Cuddy running off in the wrong direction. If he were to give him some false information, Cuddy would tell Duncan and Achan. They would get word to Master Levi. Most of them would go running off thinking they were on Phoebe's trail, giving her more time to get further away from capture. For a second, the plan sounded wonderful. Until it donned on him. He didn't know where Phoebe went. What if he mistakenly sent a whole army in her direction? He'd never be able to live with himself, especially now that he knew it was his lie that convinced her to run off.

"I said fess up!" Cuddy shouted.

"I don't know anything," Finney said.

Cuddy punched the lad in the stomach, knocking the wind out of him. "Wrong answer. Try again."

Gasping for breath and holding his stomach, Finney said, "She... didn't tell me... anything."

Cuddy grabbed a handful of Finney's hair and bent him forward. In a sudden, unexpected move, he used both arms to thrust the lad to the ground, giving Finney a mouthful of dirt. "Don't lie to me, cracker. Where was Phoebe heading?"

Rolling to his side, Finney spit as much dirt out of his mouth as possible. For the first time since Phoebe's disappearance, Finney was grateful she hadn't told him where she was going. No matter what Cuddy, or either of the other two mulattos, did to him, there was no chance he could squeal.

"Don't make me repeat the question," Cuddy said.

"I'd tell you if I knew. Honest, I would."

"On your feet," Cuddy ordered.

Nervously, Finney stood.

"If Phoebe didn't tell you anything about running, what were you secretly meeting with her about?"

Finney was quite thankful he wasn't a believer, and he still had the freedom to lie without feeling guilty about it. "We were trying to decide if we were interested in each other."

Cuddy smiled. "Interested? As in having a relationship with each other? You and that smoked Irish girl? That'd be the day."

Finney struggled to understand. Mulattos were partially Irish and partially smoked Irish. How could Cuddy be a part of the crowd who considered interracial relationships inappropriate? Still, it wasn't the time for a debate, so Finney pretended to agree. "I know. We were being foolish, and we both came to realize that."

Cuddy tightly gripped Finney's elbow, "I'm not convinced you don't know anything but there's much work to do. I'll tell you what I'm going to do. I'll give you until the sun goes down to think about it. You make sure that brain of yours is working all day long. I expect you to either remember some details that might help us find that girl or to ask around and find out who has the information I'm hunting for."

CHAPTER TWENTY-ONE

DAY OF PAIN

As cruel as it may have sounded, Finney was happy to see Achan and Cuddy dragging a young smoked Irish teenager toward the whipping post. He hoped that meant the slave had either confessed to knowing something about Phoebe's running away or that he had somehow gotten caught. If that were the case, Finney wouldn't be as likely to be tormented regarding a truth he didn't have.

Horror was written all over the smoked Irish slave's face. In less than two minutes, the mulattos removed his shirt and tied him to the post. "I don't know anything," the lad insisted.

"Our time's running out, and we're tired of playing games. You spent more time working close to that runaway than anybody else did. You best be speaking up."

The terrified smoked Irish slave was visibly trembling.

Duncan backed up and ever so slowly said in all but a whisper, "I don't know one-hundred percent for sure if you're guilty or not. We can't afford to have any slaves down, so for the time being, I'm only going to take a switch to you."

A switch? Only a switch when the white crackers were constantly having the whip taken to them? That hardly seemed fair. Then again, Finney had to admit, if even to himself, that it wasn't right for somebody to get whipped at all if there were no evidence he had committed an offense. Maybe that's why the mulattos let the lad keep his breeches on.

Duncan tore a small, thin branch off a neighboring tree. "Anything you want to tell me, Archie?" he asked while violently ripping the leaves off the branch.

At least now Finney knew the slave's name. Being close to the same age, he wished there was a way he could buddy up with Archie. But what would be the point? He wasn't meant to have friends, or close relationships of any kind with anybody. It wouldn't last. At least, that's what Darcy would have thought. She always said a person's past often predicts their future.

Archie responded with a short, "No."

Duncan drew the switch back and whacked the lad's lower back. Archie tensed but didn't scream like Finney would have had the whip hit him. As the limb hit the smoked Irish slave a second time, Archie allowed a slight groan to slip out. Still, he kept himself together.

To Finney's right, another young man, a cracker, was being dragged toward the whipping post while Archie's thrashing continued. After six or seven blows, Duncan stopped, and in a hushed voice said, "Do you want to change your story?"

"I don't have a story," Archie grumbled.

The mulatto pulled the switch back and brought it down with twice as much force as he had been, this time hitting the upper part of Archie's legs. Even though the lad's thin breeches surely cushioned the blow, Archie let out a pain-filled hiss.

After striking Archie three more times in the same vicinity, Duncan stopped. "I'm not convinced he knows anything. Get the white nigger ready while I unstrap this nigger."

Finney watched in astonishment as Archie was taken off the post and given his shirt back, while Achan and Cuddy stripped the cracker completely naked and tied him where Archie had been.

As the cracker was strapped to the post, Finney couldn't help but notice the scars across his back and legs. That man had suffered brutal whippings in the past. He was either a troublemaker or somebody had it in for him.

Once the cracker was secure, Duncan handed the switch over to Cuddy.

Cuddy smirked, "It's been a while since I've had the privilege of making you scream. If I had to choose a white nigger I enjoy whipping more than any of the others, you'd be my first pick."

"I bet he thought you'd eventually get over that," Duncan said through that wicked, low-toned chuckle of his.

"I'll never forget what you did, you filthy white nigger! How you managed to squirm your way loose the first time that whip ever hit you, I'll never understand!" Cuddy appeared downright furious, as if it had just happened. "Achan nearly killed me for not tying you up tight enough. That's okay. You're not so tough anymore, are you?"

The white cracker didn't utter a word, not that Cuddy seemed to mind. With an expression of pride on his face, the mulatto gave a practice swing, aligning the branch with the white slave's tan line. Unlike Archie, who was at least ten years younger than him, the man had zero tolerance for pain. Screaming as though someone was killing him, he jerked around like crazy, trying to free himself from the whipping post. Cuddy chuckled, "And this is yet another reason why you're my favorite! You're not getting loose this time!"

The white slave continued squirming for a full thirty seconds after the switch hit him. Newt called out to him, "Be strong, Linus." That was a brave move. Finney hoped it wouldn't result in Newt being the next one hitched up.

As soon as Linus stilled his body, Cuddy hit him again, this time just above the back of his knees, hard enough to draw blood. Linus squirmed around like a nightcrawler on a fishing hook while letting out an excruciating cry that would have caused anyone with a heart to cut him loose.

Cuddy watched with great amusement until Linus got himself together again. "You can make this a lot easier on yourself, white nigger. Tell me where Phoebe went."

Linus's body jerked around as if he'd been hit again, but his sobbing was so intense he couldn't get a word out. "Have it your way," Cuddy said before striking him just below his shoulder blades. Linus's yelping brought

Finney to tears. He didn't know how much more he could take, and he wasn't even the one being beaten.

For two hours straight, slave after slave was tied to the whipping post and viciously interrogated in front of the rest of the slaves. every smoked Irish was whipped shirtless, with his breeches on, while every white slave was whipped completely bare.

Kit was up next. Even though Finney knew his friend could handle more pain than practically anyone there, he couldn't bear to watch him go through it again. Especially not after recently volunteering to take another slave's punishment.

With his heart racing, Finney said, "Stop. I'll tell you where she went."

Achan cracked a smile. "It's about time," he said. "But don't think we're going to whip the rest of these slaves for the information you've been withholding, and that a simple confession will get you off the hook. Get him up here. He can confess while I'm taking the switch to him."

Somehow Finney wasn't surprised.

Duncan and Cuddy grabbed Finney and aggressively stripped his clothes off before Duncan threw him over his shoulder and carried him to the whipping post. Finney hated the humiliation, but it wasn't nearly as bad since so many others had gone before him, and if nothing else, at least this time, he wasn't going to be facing the whip. A switch he could handle.

Once tied to the post, Finney immediately started talking, hoping to lighten the punishment. "Phoebe told me-"

"Close that mouth," Achan said before bringing the switch down a dozen times in rapid succession, striping him from shoulders to knee. None of the mulattos had whipped anyone else in the same fashion. Finney screamed. That switch hurt almost as bad as the whip. There was no way he could hold the tears back.

Achan struck him again, twice as hard as before, and said, "Now, what was it you wanted to tell us?"

Sniffling, Finney said, "Phoebe... told me... she was going to-"

The switch tore into Finney's lower back, cutting him off mid-sentence. Finney yelped.

"You were saying?" Achan laughed, hitting him again in the exact same spot.

Finney's tears went from single droplets to streams pouring out of both eyes. The switch cut into his behind before he could get another word out, forcing him to let out another yelp. "She's," the lad sniffled, "hiding... in the... woods."

Achan brought a series of at least ten more rapid succession blows to his rear end, lower back, and upper legs. "In the woods, *where?*"

Trembling, Finney said, "She headed into the woods... behind the woodshed. She said she would try to sleep in hollow logs."

The sound of an approaching horse startled Achan. The crowd grew silent. Master Levi Stone rode up and stopped just short of Finney. Finney gave him a pitiful look, hoping for mercy. Now he would find out whether or not he was right about the planter being his uncle and now recognizing him as kin. He could only hope he was right and that Master Levi would get him off of that post.

"Did he confess to anything?" Master Levi asked.

Finney was nervous.

Achan said, "Yes, sir. She's hiding in the woods. This cracker said she went out behind the woodshed, and we can find her sleeping in a hollow log."

Master Levi got off the horse and approached Finney. "Based on those tears, I'd like to think you've learned your lesson and would never help another slave escape. But I'm not a very trusting person."

Finney wanted to tell Master Levi he'd lied, but he couldn't bring himself to do it.

Master Levi pulled a whip off of his horse. Finney cringed. "Please, no, sir!"

Achan laughed. "Can I do it?" he asked.

Master Levi smiled, "It looks like you've had enough fun. I feel like I should handle this one myself."

"Yes, sir," Achan said, stepping back.

It was rare for Master Levi Stone to whip a slave himself. As a matter of fact, Finney had never seen him do it. Finney tried to convince himself it was an act of mercy. That Master Levi Stone would take it easier on him than the mulattos would have, with them being related and all.

Master Levi backed up a couple of feet, raised the whip high in the air, and struck the ground next to Finney's right foot with it. "You lied, you filthy white nigger!"

Whether he and the planter were kin or not, Finney was terrified. How did Master Levi know he'd made up the whole story?

"Do you want to admit it?"

"Yes, sir. I lied," Finney said.

Master Levi tore Finney's flesh near the midpoint of his back. Finney screamed louder than anyone had all day. That switch didn't hurt anywhere nearly as badly as the whip did. How had Finney forgotten that pain so soon?

Master Levi was furious, "Why did you make up such a tale?"

Sobbing much harder than before, Finney said, "So... nobody else," he sniffled, "would have to... have the switch taken to them."

Master Levi laughed before giving him three more lashes and saying, "Phoebe has been found, and she will not be returning to the plantation."

Finney didn't know what to make of that. Had she been sold? Found dead? Or killed for running away? He was in no position to ask.

CHAPTER TWENTY-TWO

MOVING IN

Entering the white nigger cabin again for the first time in months was a dream come true, even if the smoked Irish and mulatto slaves now had individual family shacks while the crackers still had to share a larger one. Anything was better than spending another night outside.

Finney was surprised to find the cabin practically spotless. He wasn't sure he or the other white slaves would have cleaned the quarters had the situation been reversed. In one way, it seemed like an incredibly generous gesture. In another, like a complete waste of time. Knowing his fellow slaves, Finney doubted the place would stay clean for long.

Before the lad could make his way to his bed, someone shoved him from behind. He turned to find William glaring at him. "Nice to be back indoors, isn't it?"

"It is," Finney hesitantly agreed.

"If you want to stay inside, you will learn to keep that mouth shut from the time I lay down until the time I get up. If you do anything to make me lose as much as a wink of sleep tonight, you're going to be right back outside, all by your lonesome. Understood?"

"I'll be quiet," Finney said.

"One way or another, you will be." William turned to Kit. "Same goes for you, lad. My sleep will not be disturbed by either of you." William raised his voice, "For that matter, I will not tolerate my sleep being disturbed by anyone in this cabin tonight. Don't believe me? Make a sound while I'm trying to sleep and you'll find out if I'm bluffing!"

What a joy sucker! At a time when all of the white crackers should have been rejoicing, how could William be so obnoxious? It didn't matter. Not to Finney, and apparently not to anyone else. Within seconds, it seemed like everybody in the cabin was busying about trying to get themselves settled back in.

Well, not quite everybody. Cherish laid down just inside the doorway, sobbing. Newt knelt next to her, rubbing her back. "I understand how you feel," he told her. "I miss Henry too. But behaving like this isn't going to bring him back."

Cherish went on bawling as if her husband hadn't spoken a word. Finney missed Henry too. But that's not why he started crying — watching a momma grieving the loss of her child four months after his death was heart-wrenching.

Finney watched Newt's feeble attempts at calming his wife down go on for nearly ten minutes before Kit involved himself. Finney wished he only had half of that lad's wisdom.

Kit sat on the floor next to Cherish's face. "Ma'am," he said softly. "It wasn't your fault. You were the best momma Henry could have ever asked for." Kit reached down and squeezed Cherish's hand. "Henry's a lucky lad to have you and Newt for parents. You did right by him."

Cherish returned the hand squeeze, weeping even louder. Newt stood and walked outside while Kit continued holding her hand. "Ma'am," he said, barely loud enough to be heard over her crying. "Ma'am, you were working alongside the rest of us, trying to keep as many folks alive as you could. Accidents happen. It was nobody's fault."

For a few minutes, Kit allowed Cherish to cry without interruption. Then he said, "Have you thought about where Henry is now? He's in Heaven with Jesus, and up there nobody's gonna take the whip to him. You hear me? Nobody's gonna smack your boy around; he's not going to be a slave anymore. And someday, you'll get to go there and see him."

Cherish turned her face to look up at Kit. Smiling through her tears, she said, "If your momma could see you now, she'd be proud, Kit. You're becoming quite the gentleman." With that, Cherish calmed her crying.

After watching everything in silence while trying to hide his tears, Finney turned to face the wall. Cherish was right. Kit's momma would have been proud of him. Someday, if Finney ever had children, he hoped to have a son like Kit – a lad who always did the right thing, no matter what anyone else thought of him.

"Can I pray with you?" Kit asked.

By now, Finney no longer found Kit's prayers so odd or annoying. As always, he listened in. "Dear God," Kit began. "We'd like to thank you for allowing us to know Henry for a little while. Thank You for bringing him home before anything bad could happen to him down here. Lord, please help Newt and Cherish get through their pain. They need you, Lord. We ask this in Jesus' name. Amen."

For a moment, the shack was silent. Then Kit said, "Let me help you up, Cherish."

Finney turned back to face them just as Kit stood to his feet and extended his hand. Cherish grabbed hold of his arm and pulled herself up. Once on her feet, she wrapped her arms around Kit. "You have to be the kindest young man I've ever met," she told him. "I sure wish I could have had a chance to meet your parents."

"I wish a lot of things about my parents too," he told her.

"Really? I don't know that I've ever heard you talk about them."

Finney hadn't given it much thought, but as much as he and Kit had talked, he had never heard him mention his family at all. He wondered if he would now that somebody was asking about them.

For a moment, Kit was quiet. Then he said something that shocked Finney. "I wish my mother wouldn't have convinced my father to let me get away with so much. You have no idea how many times I can remember my father getting ready to come down hard on me, and my mother saying, "Stop it. He's only a child and he'll grow out of it. He knows what he did was wrong, and feels bad enough about it as it is. All punishing him is going to do is send him a message that we don't love him. Is that what you want to do?' I developed some rotten habits because my father allowed my mother to prevent him from punishing me when I needed it."

Now that was something Finney never thought he'd hear a lad say. Kit wished his parents had punished him more? Most kids, Finney included, wanted more freedom to do what they wanted. Not more restrictions and discipline.

"But look how you turned out," Cherish said. "You're one of, if not the best-behaved lad I've ever met. Your parents must have done a fine job of raising you."

Kit grew silent again. But not for long. "I'm not like I am because of my parents. I'm like this because I asked Jesus into my heart when I was on that ship heading here. The more I prayed during that voyage, and the more verses the slave next to me quoted from the Bible, the more God softened my heart."

What? Finney could hardly believe his ears. Here he had told Kit so much about himself. Yet up until now Kit's past had been kept a complete secret from him, and he'd never even realized it. Why was that? Was it because Kit hadn't wanted to talk about it until now? Or was it something else? Finney tried to remember if he had ever asked Kit anything about his past. As far as he could recall, he never had. Maybe he had been too wrapped up in his own emotional rollercoaster to ever ask Kit how he was doing.

"That's powerful," Cherish told him. "I'm curious. What else do you wish about your parents?"

"I wish they weren't in Hell," Kit said, looking down at his feet.

"Oh, baby," Cherish said, wrapping an arm around him. "What makes you think your parents are in Hell?"

"I don't just think they are in Hell. They are in Hell. A preacher came to our house the very night they died. He asked me to stay out on the porch while he visited with my folks, and I did, but I listened in from the porch. The preacher told them they, along with everybody else who was ever born, were guilty of sin. And that their sin was the reason they needed a Savior. That accepting Jesus was the only way they could go to Heaven. My parents gave the man a hard time. My father said, "Preacher, I too once had an imagination. I used to have imaginary friends. Three of them to be exact. I would talk to them everywhere I went, as long as nobody else was around. But I grew up. Somewhere around the age of six or seven, I had to admit to myself that those friends didn't really exist. It's time for you to realize this Jesus you keep talking about was once a part of somebody else's imagination. They shared it with somebody who wrote stories about Him. Other people read those stories, and told other people about them. The whole thing is a made-up tale so people will feel better when they die, or when they see other people they love die. Sorry, preacher. I'm not talking to your imaginary friend.'

"My mother was just as bad. She said 'You're only about the fifth person who has come in here trying to convince me I need to be saved before I die. I've heard it all before, preacher. I can have eternal life if only I believe. If I don't ask Jesus into my heart, I'll burn in Hell forever. How can anyone expect me to believe that? Nothing burns forever. Throw a log on the fire, and watch how long it burns. For that matter, throw a dead rat on one. It's flesh, just like you and I are. It won't burn forever. And to believe somebody died because of bad things I did? But that they did it before I was even born and hadn't done anything wrong? Don't you see how ridiculous this is?'

"Cherish, none of us knew that was going to be their last day on earth. At the time, I had no idea if the preacher was right or if my parents were. But in the middle of that very night, both my mother and my father fell asleep on earth and woke up in Hell. I wish it weren't so. But I can't do anything to change it now."

Not wanting to hear anything else, Finney got up and walked outside. Whether Heaven and Hell existed or not, he didn't know. But Kit sure seemed confident he knew what he was talking about. Then again, it sounded like Kit's parents were every bit as sure of their own beliefs as Finney was about his. Somebody had to be right, and somebody had to be wrong. If only there was a way to know what was true!

CHAPTER TWENTY-THREE

POOR HEALTH

Finney didn't care how many times Newt said nothing was wrong. The man was seriously ill.

Newt held his head with his left hand while pulling weeds with his right. His face was as white as a sheet. "You sure you don't want me to get Master Levi?" Finney asked.

"Wouldn't do any good," Newt said. "As long as I'm breathing, Master Levi will keep me working."

Finney would take that statement as an admission that Newt was in poor health. Recognizing the, "Can't you just leave me alone" tone of the man's voice, Finney didn't respond. Instead, he continued working while watching Newt from the corner of his eye. The man had sweat dripping from his face. He was unsuccessfully attempting to suppress a horrible cough.

Whatever Newt had, Finney didn't want to catch it. Trying not to be too obvious, he slowly yet steadily moved further down the field. Before long, he was working close to Kit, who was also having difficulty not watching Newt.

"You noticed too, huh?" Finney asked.

"How could I not?" Kit replied. "He's acting just like Ms. Smith did when she died of typhoid fever."

Finney had never heard of that before. Not that he would ever admit such a thing. "It's not typhoid fever," he argued.

Kit gave him a questioning look, "What is it then?"

Glancing over at Newt, Finney saw the man furiously scratching his belly. "I'd say it's smallpox."

Achan appeared out of nowhere, "You crackers aren't supposed to be talking. Close those mouths and get to work. Got me?"

Achan glared at Newt. "You, there! Stop slacking off, and pick up the pace!"

Finney and Kit watched to see how Newt might respond. The man reached for another handful of weeds but fell on his face. Newt didn't move. The lads feared he was dead.

Apparently, Achan didn't see things the same way the lads did. "Get up, you lazy white nigger," he insisted while stomping toward the unconscious slave.

"He's sick," Kit said. Finney wondered what it would take for his friend to learn his lesson. Sometimes he thought the lad enjoyed getting himself into trouble.

"I'll deal with you in a minute," Achan said while continuing his march toward Newt. "Did you not hear me, white nigger?" He kicked Newt in the side. "You can't be sleeping on the job!"

"I said he's sick," Kit repeated.

Achan glared at Kit while kicking Newt a second time. When Newt didn't move, the man leaned over and placed two fingers on the side of his neck. Without a word, he left Newt lying there and proceeded toward Kit.

Finney cringed in fear. He couldn't stand the idea of Kit getting another beating. On the other hand, Kit had a look of peaceful satisfaction on his face. It was almost as if he were about to receive a reward for some great deed he'd accomplished.

Achan jerked the hoe out of Kit's hand, drew it back, and hit him in the chest with it. Kit stumbled backward a few steps. Raising the hoe above his head, Achan charged at Kit. Kit ducked, trying to avoid the blow, causing the hoe handle to hit him upside the head. Kit fell limp, and Finney watched in horror.

Achan threw the hoe down and glared at Finney. "Get to work, cracker, or you'll be next."

Finney desperately wanted to check on his friend. But he couldn't. Not if he wanted to reach adulthood.

Achan knelt next to him, put two fingers on the side of his neck as he had done with Newt, looked around, and hoisted Kit up over his shoulder. "Not a word to anyone," he said, staring Finney in the eye before walking off.

Chapter Twenty-Four

An Unruly Tongue

Whatever that heavenly aroma was, it was difficult for Finney to ignore, especially while working with an empty stomach. Raising his head and sniffing the air for at least the twentieth time in the past five minutes, he was certain he'd never smelled anything so divine!

Finney looked around. All of the other slaves were working every bit as hard as they ever did. It was as though he was the only one being taunted by what smelled like a feast made for kings. But how could that even be possible?

Glancing over, the lad noticed Newt was coming back to. At least he was still alive! While pulling weeds, Finney watched as the man's eyes widened and a confused expression appeared on his face. "What happened?" he asked, looking at Finney.

Finney put a finger over his lips, "We've got to keep it down. But you were sweating really bad and fell over."

"You mean I passed out?" Newt rolled onto his belly and carefully rose to his knees. "Has Master Levi seen me?"

"No, sir," Finney said.

"How about Cherish?"

"No, sir. Just me, Kit, and Achan. Are you feeling better?"

"I feel fine," Newt said. "Looks like Master Levi's heading this way, though. Let's quit talking before we both get hitched up to that whipping post."

Finney wasn't about to argue with that. Not only was he terrified of that whip, but he didn't think Newt's body could withstand a beating in his condition.

Master Levi had that all too familiar scowl on his face as he approached. Finney tried to keep his eyes on his work, but that was all but impossible. "Two more wasted sterlings," he grumbled. Stopping practically on top of Finney, he continued, "One white nigger drowns, a smoked Irish runs away, and now you go and kill another white nigger!"

"Me?" Finney gasped. "I didn't kill anybody."

Master Levi ordered Finney to drop the hoe and look him in the eye. "You cost me a lot of money today, you filthy white nigger. This plantation can't survive without enough laborers, and now we're down three. What do you suppose I should do about that?"

Finney gave Newt a pleading look. Surely the man would come to his aid in a time such as this. But he didn't. Newt continued working as if nothing was going on.

"Answer me, you white nigger!" Master Levi demanded.

Finney felt weakness in his knees. Master Levi hadn't asked him whether or not he took anybody's life. All he asked was what he should do about it. That was the only question he would answer. "I don't know, sir."

"You don't know? Use that thick head of yours. Put yourself in my shoes! If you were the plantation owner, what would you do?"

What a repulsive thought! Finney couldn't begin to fathom taking on such a role. "I... I..." the lad stammered. "I would... I wouldn't be a plantation owner."

Master Levi looked up at the sun for a moment before glaring at Finney again. "I know white niggers can't be plantation owners. What I'm asking you to do is pretend you're not a white nigger. Are you smart enough to do that?"

So many words ran through Finney's mind that he wasn't sure what to say. Plantation owners were greedy, self-centered, ungrateful barbarians. They were more heartless than anyone the lad had ever met in Dublin. But saying any of that would not go over well.

Master Levi smacked him across the face with an open palm. "Stop wasting my time, and give me an answer. What would you do if you were in my shoes?"

That did it! If the man wanted an honest answer, Finney would give him just that. So, what if he ended up on that whipping post again! "If I were in your shoes, Master Levi Stone, I'd apologize to every last one of my slaves for the way I'd been mistreating them, I'd order them to strip me naked, strap me to the whipping post, and insist each one of them give me a dozen lashes with the horsewhip, and after that, I'd set them all free. Starting with the one related to me."

Finney hadn't meant to utter that last sentence. But he certainly couldn't do anything to take it back.

Newt looked up. With a grin on his face, he gave Finney a wink that said, "That took some guts, lad. I'm proud of you."

Master Levi stared at Finney blankly for a moment. Then he did that which was unexpected. He laughed. Not a fake one either. The man laughed so hard a tear rolled down his cheek.

Cautiously, Finney gave him a half-smile.

"When I came over here, I had every intention of whipping a white nigger within an inch of his life. And believe me, you deserve just that! But you just redeemed yourself, lad. I haven't seen anyone with so much bravery in many years. Get back to work, and we'll forget it. It's not like I paid much for the poor white nigger anyhow or like he can't be replaced."

Smiling, Finney complied. But he couldn't help notice Master Levi hadn't denied their kinship. That man had to be Uncle Keir. He just had to be. Eventually, Finney hoped the man would admit who he really was.

In the meantime, the planter's accusation kept replaying in his mind. Why did Master Levi say he had killed another white nigger? Suddenly he caught another whiff of that scrumptious smell. Oh, how he hoped whatever was being prepared was for everybody, and not just for the mulattos and the smoked Irish.

Once the planter was out of earshot, Newt said, "Finney, I'm a little concerned about you right now. You told me you don't know where Kit is, and then Master Levi comes over here saying you killed one of his white slaves? What is it you're not telling me. Where's your friend?"

"I don't know. Achan beat on him, and he fell to the ground. He wasn't moving, just like you weren't. Achan carried him off someplace. I'm hoping he'll wake back up like you did and they'll bring him back over here to the field. But Achan put a couple of fingers on the side of his neck before carrying him away. Any idea what that means?"

"That explains it," Newt said.

"Explains what?"

"You didn't notice that smell, did you, Finney?"

The smell? The scrumptious meal smell? Newt smelled it too. At least the lad knew he wasn't crazy.

Newt continued, "Kit's been killed. I hate to tell you this, but what you smell is your friend's body being burned to ashes."

Finney's eyes widened, "Are you sure?"

Newt punched the ground. "There's no doubt in my mind! Another white slave's died young. And they always burn the bodies. I'm sorry, lad."

Finney thought he was going to be sick. Why did everyone he ever got close to have to die? And worse, how could he have found the smell of his best friend's burning flesh appetizing?

CHAPTER TWENTY-FIVE

REPLACEMENTS COMING

It had been twenty-four hours, and Finney's insides were still in knots. Not only had Newt passed out, Achan murdered Kit and blamed Finney for his crime, but Finney had said awful things to his master and managed to get away with it.

Newt was steadily working three rows over from Finney. The man intentionally kept himself away from the other slaves as his illness worsened. He had thrown up at least five times during the last hour, and every time he did, Finney nearly gagged.

Finney didn't understand how anyone as physically weak as Newt could work so hard. The lad couldn't help but peek over at Newt every couple of minutes, half expecting him to fall into a state of unconsciousness as he had the day before. Newt regularly wiped the sweat from his brow, held onto his stomach, and let out agonizing groans, but not once did he take a break.

Cherish worked in a row between the two of them. "Are you doing okay?" she whispered from time to time.

Each time she asked, Newt gave her the same reply, "I'm still breathing."

Cherish looked worried, but other than frequently checking on her man, she didn't speak a word to anybody. Not that she ever did when working those fields. Finney didn't know if she was so focused on the labor that she didn't think about talking or if she was too afraid of what might happen to her if she didn't get enough work done.

Either way, Finney knew she wouldn't appreciate it if he tried to strike up a conversation.

The plantation was becoming a lonely place now that Phoebe and Kit were gone and Newt was feeling so down. Finney sure hoped that man pulled through. He dreaded the thought of another loss.

Master Levi Stone and Duncan were slowly walking the field's length. Finney couldn't help but overhear their conversation when they got close. Duncan was saying, and strangely enough, at a normal volume, and at a regular pace, "We're workin' them as hard as we can, but we're down too many."

"Agreed," Master Levi said. "Unfortunately, there aren't any slave auctions coming up in the near future. Tomorrow, I'm leaving you in charge of the plantation. I'm going to go around to the neighbors to see if I can't talk anybody into selling."

Duncan sounded disappointed. "I guess we don't have much choice," he said. "It's just that every time we go that route, we end up getting the troublemakers. That's all anybody wants to sell."

More slaves? Finney wasn't sure what to think of that idea. In a way, it would be nice to no longer be the new guy. On the other hand, the idea of some new troublemakers coming to the property sounded good. Maybe one of them would be an escape artist he could learn a few tricks from, if not team up with.

Finney sure wished Master Levi and Duncan had stopped walking and continued their conversation where he could clearly hear the whole thing. At least he heard the juicy part before they moved on.

Finney glanced over at Cherish. She didn't have to say anything. The expression on her face made it clear she'd heard everything Finney had.

For a few seconds, Finney imagined how Kit would have reacted to such news. He'd have started praying right then and there, no doubt asking God to show mercy on whoever was chosen to join the unpaid workforce of Master Levi Stone.

Finney still wished he knew if God were real and if prayer-poems really worked. Darcy always said prayer was a way for weak people to make themselves feel better about difficulties they were facing. Kit probably wouldn't have gotten along very well with her. Oh, how Finney would like to hear the two of them debate their beliefs!

Wait a minute! Was Master Levi really going to a slave auction? Or was he about to take off on one of those secret trips he was accustomed to taking? Perhaps he was going to use a slave auction to cover his tracks. If Master Levi were really Uncle Keir and he was going back to do some business in Dublin, he could be gone for months!

CHAPTER TWENTY-SIX

STARE OF DEATH

Newt was working much slower than he had on previous days. His skin was paler and his breathing far shallower. With Achan heading their direction, Newt forced himself to yank out another clump of weeds.

Finney watched Achan through the corner of his eye while continuing to work harder than he ever had.

Achan approached Newt, "You've been slacking off all day, you filthy white nigger. On those feet! Come with me!"

Newt struggled to stand, appearing as though he might pass out at any second. He gazed creepily at Finney while walking toward Achan. If the lad had ever seen a stare of death, that was it!

Cherish, acting entirely out of character, ran across the field. "My husband is ill!" she shouted. "He's doing the best he can. Now you leave him alone!"

Achan laughed while playing with his whip. "Sounds to me like both of you need a good whipping."

If anybody needed a good thrashing, it was Achan. Too bad nobody asked Finney what he thought. The lad gave Achan a dirty look. One day he hoped somebody would get the upper hand on that mulatto. And he hoped it would happen sooner rather than later.

Out of nowhere, Jane piped up, "I overheard Newt and Cherish talking in the cabin this morning. Cherish told him to exaggerate his illness today so he could get some extra rest. The only reason she's throwing such a fit now is because she feels guilty that her plan backfired and got her man in trouble. She doesn't want him to be upset with her for the beating he's about to get."

Finney was beginning to absolutely detest Lying Jane. No matter what she said, it seemed like the mulattos, and even Master Levi himself, believed her. How did they not see her for the low-down snake she was?

"Newt, Cherish, let's go!" Achan demanded.

Newt tried to push himself up off the ground, but before he could William charged furiously toward the mulatto. "If you whip either of them, you will have to whip me too!"

Surely Achan wouldn't beat a defenseless one-armed man, even if it was at that man's own suggestion. Sometimes Finney had to wonder if some of his fellow slaves ever took the time to think before they spoke.

Achan chuckled, "William, you're only saying that because you know your father won't allow me to tear your flesh. As for the rest of you, do you really think you're going to form some kind of an uprising? Not on my watch!"

His father? Who was William's father? Of everything else he'd seen and heard, that comment was one Finney couldn't ignore. William's father wouldn't allow Achan to whip him? There was only one person who could forbid a mulatto from whipping somebody. But Master Levi Stone couldn't possibly be William's father. Kit said Master Levi had gone on a long trip, and when he returned William was with him. If William was his son, he'd have been on the plantation ever since he was born. Maybe the mulatto misspoke, and meant to say "the master" instead of "your father." But it sure didn't seem that way. Nervously, Finney continued working.

Linus hollered, "How strong's your arm there, mulatto? Wanna take that whip to me as well? You whip any of them, and I'm not going to work for another minute, no matter what you do to me. You can whip me all day long if you want to. You touch them, and I'm done!"

An all-day whipping? What a dreadful thought! A part of Finney wanted to join the rebels, but he could never say the types of things they other slaves were for fear the mulattos might take him up on his offer. After everything he'd already been through himself and after everything he'd witnessed, he decided to wait. If he were meant to jump in, he would know when it was the right time.

A sinister grin took over Achan's face. "You know I'm not the only one here who has the authority to give out lashings. If I have to whip every last one of you, that's what I'm going to do."

Harriet spoke with a trembling voice, "Master Levi wouldn't be pleased if he comes back and finds none of his slaves able to work."

The mulatto stormed toward her. As he did, an entire field of slaves came running at Achan. It was time! Finney jumped up and joined their ranks. Not one white slave stayed in their position working the field.

Achan looked terrified. "String him up!" one of the white crackers called.

"Get his clothes off first!" another one shouted. "Let's give him a dose of his own medicine!"

Finney couldn't believe what was taking place. He was actually a part of a mob. And it was going to be fun to see Achan get what he had coming to him. In one accord, the group ran upon the man, knocked him to the ground, and began ripping off his clothes. Finney hoped he would be given an opportunity to crack that whip himself.

Once Achan was completely undressed, the mob forced him toward the whipping post. Before they could get him secured to it, however, Duncan came running. He clapped his hands and shouted, "Stop this at once!"

For a second, the mob grew quiet. Then one of the white crackers hollered, "He can go next!" The crowd went wild!

Cuddy came into view. He hollered something at the smoked Irish who were still working in a nearby field. Finney couldn't make out what was being said, but at a moment's notice, the plantation broke out in a war.

The smoked Irish charged at the whites and freed the mulattos from the mob. Something hit Finney in the back of the head. Everything went black.

CHAPTER TWENTY-SEVEN

NEWCOMERS

Waking up underwater was anything but a pleasant experience. Finney's eyes and mouth popped open simultaneously. In no time, his head was above the water's surface, and he broke into a hysterical fit of coughing. Duncan glared at him from the bank. "Get up here, you filthy white nigger," he said, dragging out each word with a malicious smirk on his face.

Finney was more confused than ever before. The last thing he remembered was a bunch of yelling, screaming, shoving, and punching. How he ended up in the water and how everything had quieted down, the lad had no idea.

With chattering teeth, Finney made his way out of the water.

"Fortunately for you lad, Master Levi's back, and says there's not enough time to give all of you white niggers the whippings you've earned. Instead, you'll have no food for the next forty-eight hours. Get to the field! If you join an uprising like that again, you won't get off quite so easy."

Finney wasted no time in heading to the field. On his way there, the lad heard a young girl scream as Achan pressed a branding iron tight against her arm. Three young ladies were standing in line behind her awaiting their turn. An older teenage boy was being secured to the whipping post and in line behind him were several other new male slaves, all of which had freshly burned brandmarks on their behinds.

"Move it!" Duncan said quietly but firmly. "Enough time has been wasted here today! Get moving or I'll get Master Levi's permission to secure you to that post after it gets dark tonight."

"Yes, sir," Finney said, feeling sorry for the new slaves and wishing there was something he could do to stop that barbaric practice from unfolding.

As he got closer to the field, he heard the young man on the whipping post let out a horrendous scream. The beating was beginning, and nothing could be done about it. Finney cringed, somehow feeling as though he were the one getting the lashing.

Ahead of the lad, Cherish was furiously pulling weeds with tears streaming down her face. She worked harder and faster than Finney had ever seen her work.

Finney scanned the field. There, on the ground right next to it, laid Newt. His face was bloody, and his eyes wide. Finney stopped in his tracks. Before the lad had time to even think on what he was seeing, a whip cut into his back. Taken by surprise, Finney yelped in pain.

"Get to work!" Duncan ordered in that breathy whisper of his. "I'm not going to say it again!"

Finney could feel his blood soaking into his shirt. It hurt, but he knew that one lash was nothing in comparison to the treatment the new slaves were getting. He hadn't forgotten the hospitality Kit had shown him his first night there. He didn't know how he'd repay that kindness to so many new slaves at once, but he wouldn't allow Kit's death to be in vain. He would carry on where his friend had left off.

Without looking back at Duncan, Finney continued toward the field, eyeing Newt as he went. The man showed no sign of life. No blinking, no fidgeting, his chest didn't move up or down. There was no doubt about it. Newt had been killed. Who did it or why, Finney didn't know. But now, he understood that evil glint in Cherish's eye. She had likely witnessed the whole attack from start to finish. First Henry, then Kit, who had shown her so much kindness when she was mourning the loss of her little boy, and now her husband.

Cherish threw her hands up in the air. "God!" she said loudly. "Why couldn't Master Levi have left William on the other plantation with Mistress Edith? Newt would still be alive!"

"Stop that!" Duncan said in an agitated murmur. "Don't you dare complain about Master Levi or William. And don't be blaming William for what happened to Newt. Newt died because he chose to rebel against his authority figure. He fought against the correction I attempted to give him. You saw the whole thing. He tried to attack me, and William came to my defense. Now you quit all of that blubbering and get to work!"

Chapter Twenty-Eight

DOC FINNEY

What a sight! Blood-streaked white bodies decorated the cabin floor, and pain-filled moanings and groanings echoed off the walls.

While most of the seasoned slaves silently stepped across the newcomers' backs and made their way either to their beds or the kitchen table, Finney sat on his knees between a couple of the new guys.

Not caring how the other slaves might react, he said, "What Master Levi and the mulattos did to you was horrible, and I would have stopped them if I knew how. They did the same thing to me several months ago." None of the new slaves looked at him. Finney couldn't blame them. They had no idea who they could or couldn't trust. For all they knew, he could be Master Levi's son, aiming to report whatever they said or did to Master Levi.

Finney couldn't ask Newt to gather water like Cherish had done for him in the past. Nor could the lad expect Cherish to help out while dealing with her own grief. "I'll be right back."

Rushing outside, Finney drew a pail of water from the well and carefully carried it back inside. The slaves who had been a part of the Stone plantation for much longer than Finney had pretended not to notice what the lad was doing.

Finney didn't care. If he had to take care of all of the new slaves by himself, he would do it. Not knowing where to find a rag, he took his shirt off and dipped it in the pail of water. "I'm going to clean up your wounds now," he told teenage lad who appeared to be a couple of years older than he was.

The lad turned to face Finney. "No need. I'll help you care for the others," he said with a voice crack. The young man slowly rose to his knees. Finney didn't know where the older teen found the strength to move, yet was inspired by the lad's selflessness.

Finney stuck out his hand and introduced himself.

The lad returned the favor, "Nice to meet you, Finney. I'm Cager. How can I help?"

"I don't know," Finney said. "I suppose we can take turns swapping positions. While one of us cleans wounds, the other can keep folks from fidgeting too much."

"I can do that," Cager said. "But you should probably know I have a weak stomach, and blood makes me squeamish. If I have to vomit, I'll run outside."

"Stuff like that doesn't bother me," Finney said. "What if I clean all of the wounds and you try to comfort people then? Would that be better?"

Cager nodded with a smile, "I appreciate that, *Doc* Finney. Should we start with this guy right here?"

If he weren't so busy, Finney would have found the Doc comment funny. Instead of laughing though, he looked at the fellow lying next to him and said, "Looks like as good of a place to start as any."

Cager placed a gentle hand on the man's head. "My friend Finney here is going to clean you up," he said softly. "It's going to sting; there's no way around that. I want you to be strong and to lay as still as you can. Try not to yell or scream. We'll get this over with as soon as we can."

Finney smiled when Cager referred to him as a friend. Putting that thought aside, he dipped his shirt in the water, and lightly dabbed a cut in the center of the man's back. The cracker didn't move, except for squinting his eyes. In less than thirty seconds, Finney's shirt was covered in blood. He dipped it back in the water and cleaned it off as best as possible before wiping away more blood.

For two hours, Finney and Cager tended the other new slaves. Once they were finished, Finney said, "It's your turn, Cager. Lay down so I can clean you up."

Cager shook his head. "No, thank you. I'm not comfortable having somebody touch me like that."

Finney chuckled, "Is it comfortable having blood ooze all down the back of you?"

"Good point, but there has to be another way."

"Like what?" Finney asked. "If we go out to the creek at this time of night and somebody catches us, we're going to be in a lot of trouble."

"Give me your shirt," Cager said. "Let me clean up whatever I can reach, and I'll let you clean up what I can't."

CHAPTER TWENTY-NINE

THE REBEL

Cherish didn't sleep off her anger. Anyone with half a brain could see she was not in her normal state of mind. "Leave me alone!" she snapped at Cuddy. "I'm working as hard as I can."

Finney knew Cherish was going to be in trouble with that attitude. He was right too! Cuddy shoved the newly widowed woman. She stumbled backward but maintained her balance. Glaring at the mulatto, she said, "You ought to be ashamed of yourself! Doing Master Levi's dirty work makes you every bit as evil as he is."

Cuddy smacked her face with the back of his hand. Finney looked around, fully expecting an army of resistance from the other white slaves who certainly heard, if not saw, everything that was taking place. Yet, none opened their mouths or stepped forward to defend her.

Finney glanced ahead to see how Cager might react to such a thing. The lad kept his eyes focused on the field in front of him. It was obvious he was purposefully not looking in Cherish's direction.

Unphased by Cuddy's harsh treatment, Cherish stared him straight in the eye and said, "I was getting a lot more work done before you started harassing me. Look how much time you're wasting!"

Cuddy did something Finney hadn't seen done before. He waved his arm high in the air while looking off into the distance. Finney followed his gaze. The man was drawing the attention of Master Levi.

Continuing to work the field, Finney quietly watched as Cuddy and Cherish stared each other down until Master Levi arrived. "What seems to be the trouble?" he asked.

"She's trying to bring the kind of issues we had yesterday," Cuddy said. "She refuses to work and is doing everything she can to get the others in an uproar."

Cherish crossed her arms while glaring at both of them.

Master Levi instructed Cuddy to seize her. "Use whatever force necessary to get her to the whipping post. I'll be there with further instructions momentarily. First, I'd like to have a word with the rest of these white niggers."

Cherish took off running, but Cuddy was too fast for her. In less than thirty seconds, he caught up to her, wrapped an arm around her neck, and forced her out of the field. Master Levi didn't speak until they were well out of earshot. "I thought I made myself clear yesterday. Some of you white niggers seem to think you're above the law. I paid good money for each and every one of you, but that doesn't mean I value your lives. From now on, anyone who refuses instruction will suffer the same fate as that woman."

No one spoke.

Master Levi looked around for a moment before locking his eyes on Cager. "You, white nigger," he said. "Come with me. I want you to witness everything that takes place. As soon as her punishment is through, I want you to return here, tell the others what you saw, and get back to work."

"Yes, sir," Cager replied.

Finney was nervous for yet jealous of Cager at the same time. As little desire as he had to witness any more violence, Finney wanted to be the first to know what happened to Cherish especially since he saw her as somewhat of a second mother figure.

"Cuddy, grab that rebellious white nigger and bring her to the whipping post." Pointing to the far end of the field, Master Levi addressed the rest of the white slaves, "Achan will be keeping an eye on you from a distance. If any of you get out of line, you'll soon wish you hadn't."

Twenty minutes passed between the time Master Levi and Cager left the field and the time when Cherish's blood-curdling screams filled the plantation. Finney was torn. Kit's words were coming back to haunt him. After all Cherish had done, he should be doing something to take care of her. Something to suggest at least a hint of gratefulness. But it was too late for that. They were too far away. He could never get that far without Achan stopping him. Even if he could, there was no way he could stop Master Levi and Cuddy from whipping her.

Another scream met his ear. Finney's body trembled uncontrollably. He knew that kind of pain. He could imagine Cuddy smiling as Master Levi swung the whip. He could feel that cruel instrument cutting into his flesh. Tears rolled down his cheeks as his pulse raced. Oh, if there was something he could do to help her. Maybe volunteer to take the rest of her beating? No. He could never bring himself to do that. Not even for Cherish. Even the thought of such an act overwhelmed the lad with fear.

The screaming continued for what seemed like an eternity before things eventually grew quiet. He could now only hope Cager would really return to tell them what happened. And hopefully, if things went well, Cherish would make her way to the field once she regained enough strength to do so.

Waiting on Cager's report was the most difficult part of the entire ordeal. So many thoughts raced through Finney's mind. What if he had done something during Cherish's whipping that upset Master Levi or Cuddy? For all he knew, they were in the process of hitching him to the whipping post. Surely not so soon after his welcome-to-the-plantation beating!

Finney tried to busy himself pulling weeds, but his fingers didn't want to cooperate. If he weren't afraid of what Achan would do to him, he'd sprawl out there on the ground and not move until he found out if Cherish and Cager were okay. Finney put both hands on top of his head and took a deep breath. He had to calm himself down somehow.

Thankfully, he saw Cager running his way. Finney couldn't take his eyes off the lad. Cager's eyes were filled with tears of hysteria. Wiping his face and hesitantly looking back toward the whipping post, he said, "The mulatto beat her until she stopped screaming. Then they lit her hands and feet on fire. They didn't stop there. They burned her alive."

"Burned her alive?" Harriet shrieked. "Cherish is dead?"

"Yes, ma'am," Cager said. "If she's saved, she's in Heaven with Jesus."

"I'm not sure how much more of this I can take," Harriet fumed. "I feel like it's every day anymore that somebody's getting beaten or burned or killed."

"Sometimes I think I'd rather be beaten or burned than treated the way I am," William interrupted.

Finney was surprised to hear William jump into such a conversation. He knew if he spoke, he'd likely only make William furious so he decided to stay out of it, while hoping somebody would engage him.

But they didn't. For several minutes, not another word was spoken. What could William possibly have meant? It wasn't like anyone was mistreating him! Finney couldn't let it go. Even though it would prove a horrible lack of judgement on his part, he said, "William, can I ask you a question."

"That all depends on what it is."

"What did you mean about wishing you'd get beaten or burned as opposed to being treated how you are now? Is somebody treating you bad?"

William sighed. "You know what? I don't care what he does to me. He can ship me back to my mother's start-up plantation if he wants to. I am a person too, and I should be able to share my story just like everybody else does!"

"What story? Like, about how you lost your arm, and how you ended up here?"

"Everything!" William said. "I'm at the place where I'm ready to talk about everything. What do you want to know? My life's an open book."

"Okay," Finney said, surprised at such an unusual conversation with William. "Who were you talking about when you said 'he can ship me back to my mother's start-up plantation?' Who do you think would ship you off somewhere? Master Levi? And if your mother has a start-up plantation, why aren't you there?"

William looked around, but the look on his face didn't say he was hoping to get away with what he was about to say. It was almost like he was hoping one of the mulattos would come close enough to hear him.

"Master Levi Stone is my father," he said.

Finney felt his jaw drop. "What? That can't be! Then why are you out here working like a slave?"

"I guess it's embarrassing to have a son with only one arm. That's why, up until now, I've never mentioned it. I was threatened not to ever tell a soul he's my father. He never said what he would do to me if I told, but he's never gotten physical with me so I'm assuming he would send me back to my mother's start-up."

Wow! Finney had trouble believing what he was hearing. But in a way, it made sense. What else would explain why the mulattos never punished him, and why Master Levi never thought he did anything wrong? Still not sure what to think, Finney asked more questions. "So, who is your mother, and where is this start-up?"

"My mother's name is Edith. The way I understand it, she and my father used to be married. They both lived here up until the time I was born. My father was so humiliated by my deformity that he didn't want anything to do with me. He felt like I was some kind of damaged product. Like I would never amount to anything. A few days after I was born, my mother walked into the room and found him with his hand covering my mouth and nose. She said he was trying to kill me. She screamed, and shoved him away from me. They got into some kind of a fight; I believe it turned physical. Master Levi gave her a choice. It was either get rid of me, or he would get rid of her."

How disgusting! What kind of man could be so cruel to his newborn child or to the mother of his baby?

William looked around again, this time looking slightly worried. "I can't believe I just told you all of that. I've never told anybody."

"It's okay," Finney said. "I can keep secrets."

"Nobody's asking you to keep secrets. As of today, I'm no longer going to hide this from anybody. It's my life, and I'm going to talk about it, regardless of the consequences."

"So, that story," Finney said, "about you losing your arm fighting with a bull? That's not true then?"

"No," William said. "I believe my father made that story up and told it to one of his mulattos, who talked about it in front of some of the smoked Irish, and word began to spread. I think my father feels like it was somehow his fault I was born this way. Like there was something wrong with him and he couldn't produce a 'normal' child. That's why he's never had more children."

"Are you sure that's why?" Finney asked.

"What other explanation could there be?"

"I don't know," Finney said. "Maybe since him and your mother got separated, he hasn't been close enough to a woman to have another baby?"

William snickered, "Master Levi's good, isn't he?"

"What do you mean?"

"You don't know that he and my mother have had an on-going relationship for years, do you?"

Finney shook his head.

"I didn't think so. You haven't heard tale of him leaving the mulattos in charge for lengthy period of times before you got here?"

"I've heard he's been gone for months at a time and nobody knew why. That's why I thought he was-" Finney stopped himself. No, he probably shouldn't go there.

"That's why you thought he was what?"

Finney took a deep breath. If William could be so forthcoming, why couldn't he? "Master Levi looks an awfully lot like my Uncle Keir. For a while I convinced myself it was him. And when people told me about some of the long trips he takes, I thought maybe he was going back and forth between here and Dublin somehow. You know, that he was living a double life maybe?"

"No chance of that," William said. "With my father, for the most part what you see is what you get. Those long trips he's taken have all been to spend time with my mother. When Master Levi told her she had to leave, he helped her get to her parents' property. Over the years, he's came out and stayed on the property for far longer than I've wanted him to. He built her a cute plantation house, and a couple of slave shacks. He's been putting fencing up all around her property. He's bought her a couple of female slaves, but fears my mother's not strong enough to keep any male slaves in line. For a while, I think he convinced himself when I got old enough, I would be able to help her out in that area, in spite of the missing arm."

"Since you're here, that means he changed his mind?"

"He did. The last time he came for a visit, him and my mother got in a big argument. The next thing I knew he ordered me to get in his cart and said I was coming to live with him. Confused, I looked at my mother. With tears rolling down her cheeks, she hugged me and said, 'Your father and I have discussed this, and we think it's best. I'm sure he'll bring you around for visits from time to time.' She told me she loved me, and that was it."

Out of nowhere, Jane interrupted, "Oh, poor, pitiful William! His father is embarrassed by him, and so we should all give him lots and lots of sympathy. Poor fellow. Do you really think you're the only one who has been warned to keep secrets or whose parents don't like them because they're different? Believe me, you're not."

Where that came from, Finney had no idea. But it was rude and uncalled for nonetheless. And for once, he was going to say so. "Jane, William never talks about anything in his life. Don't criticize him the first time he does."

"I'll criticize whoever I want to. And if I were you, I wouldn't talk to me that way. When any of the mulattos come over, guess who's going to get a whipping! Here's a hint. It won't be me."

Lying Jane was right. She, like William, never got in trouble for anything. If William was never faulted with being in the wrong because Master Levi Stone was his father, than, yes! She had to be! "Your Cuddy's daughter, aren't you?" he blurted out.

191

Jane shook her head, "I did not say that."

William smiled. "He's right, isn't he? I remember Cuddy saying his father reported that Finney and Phoebe had some alone time together right before she ran away. None of us had ever heard of him having a daughter before that day. You're Cuddy's little girl."

Jane turned her back, "Yes. Cuddy's my father."

William chuckled, "So my father all but disowned me because I'm missing an arm. You have both arms, both legs, both eyes, both ears. Everything about you looks pretty normal. Well, all but that big nose maybe."

Jane hesitantly felt her nose as William continued, "So why did your father disown you? I doubt it was because of the nose. Too much lying, maybe?"

Jane started to walk away, but William followed her. "Maybe it's because he thought you were too stupid?"

She kept walking. "Because you weren't a boy?"

Jane spun around to face him. "My mother was an Irish slave, and Cuddy didn't want anybody to know. Master Levi helped him hide the secret by selling my mother off to a different plantation before I was born. Then he 'bought' me several years later, and brought me back here because Cuddy was afraid my mother would tell me a bunch of lies about him. The truth is, I'm a mulatto but because I look white, they forced me to sleep in the white nigger cabin and to be treated pretty much like the rest of you. There! Are you happy now?"

CHAPTER THIRTY

LENDING AN EAR

Finney was beginning to understand why William got so upset when people made noise at night. Was Cager ever going to stop rolling back and forth? For once, he wanted and expected William to stop him. But he didn't. It was as if William didn't hear a thing, or as if it wasn't bothering him. After trying to ignore the constant movement for hours, Finney finally whispered, "Having trouble falling asleep?"

Cager sat up and held a finger over his lips. He stood and walked toward the door motioning for Finney to come with him. Reluctantly, Finney followed.

Once outside, Cager said, "I didn't want to take a chance on waking anybody up. My mind is going in a million directions at once. I want to sleep, but I can't."

"What are you thinking about?"

"Everything!" Cager said. "My family, the way the mulattos branded and whipped all of us the other day, what they did to Cherish, whether Cherish is in Heaven or in Hell-"

Finney cut him off, "I take it you're a believer?"

"I am," Cager said. "But I'm not the kind to force my beliefs on anybody else."

"We'll get along fine then," Finney said. "Because spiritual talk has separated friendships for me in the past."

"Sorry to hear that," Cager replied. "Are you a good listener?"

"I guess so," Finney said. "Why do you ask?"

"Don't take this as being rude, but I just need to talk and have somebody listen. You know, without passing any kind of judgment or anything. Just to let me get some things off my mind."

Finney nodded, "Go for it. I won't say a word."

"My family was homeless," Cager began. "It wasn't by choice. Nobody wanted to hire my father on account of his bum leg. Not only that, but my mother died giving birth to my little sister. So, all five of us survived by rummaging through people's garbage and asking for handouts. We lived that way for years. Some think that would be embarrassing, but for us, it was just a normal way of life.

"One day, my father met some man everybody called a spirit. He said he could help us get off the streets and make sure we didn't have to beg for food. I don't think my father understood what all the agreement entailed, but he signed off on some paperwork, and the next thing I knew, we all boarded a ship headed for the new world. On the voyage, one of my little brothers and my older sister both got sick and died. Then when we arrived here, things got downright creepy."

"What do you mean?" Finney asked.

"Me, my father, and my little sister were lined up on an auction block along with a lot of other soon-to-be indentured servants. Strangers kept coming over and inspecting us. I'm sure you've experienced that, right?"

"Twice," Finney said. "But that's just a part of the process."

"I know," Cager replied. "But when Master Levi showed up, my father seemed like he was in a state of disbelief. Like they knew each other somehow."

Finney couldn't believe what he was hearing. He cut him off, "I think I know where this is going. Levi's not his real name, is it? His real name is Keir?"

"I don't think so," Cager said. "None of us were allowed to speak. But Master Levi stood right between my father and I. He told my father it had been a while since they had seen one another. My father nodded in silence. Master Levi said, 'Remember when I told you I'd pay you back for stealing my sweetheart? We were what, about sixteen?' My father nodded again. Master Levi laughed the most wicked laugh I'd ever heard. 'It looks like I'm about to fulfill my word. But the thing is, I don't necessarily want three of you on my plantation. I'm only going to take one. The question is, should I take you?' He paused for a moment. 'Or your son here? You didn't know I knew, did you?' Master Levi took a few steps to get closer to my sister. 'Or would you rather I take your daughter?' My father shook his head violently, and said 'If you're going to take anybody, take me and leave my children alone, Levi!' Master Levi responded with that wicked laugh again."

"Before you go any further," Finney interrupted again. "Where did you live before you came here? Dublin?"

"No. Limerick. Do you know where that is?"

"I've heard of it. But I'm not real familiar with it," Finney told him. "Do you know if your father ever lived in Dublin?"

"No. He lived his entire life in Limerick until we boarded that ship and came to the new world."

"Alright," Finney said. "I didn't mean to interrupt. Please, go on with your story."

"Master Levi walked over in front of my father. Without saying a word, he moved back over and stood in front of my sister. 'Little girl, would you like to come live with me?' He asked. My sister shook her head. Master Levi asked her why. She squeaked out a, 'I'm scared and just want to go home.' So, Master Levi stepped in front of me. 'How about you, lad? I'm going to take either you, your sister, or your father to my plantation. Shall I bring you?' I didn't know what to do. I glanced over at my father and then at my sister. I was every bit as scared as my sister was. Master Levi planned to get revenge on my father. Whichever one of us he took, I assumed he was going to torture, and possibly even kill. There was no way I could let my sister go with him. But if I let my father go, he'd certainly be mistreated far worse than me or my sister would be. So, I thought it only logical for me to go. With tears in my eyes, I nodded and told him I was willing to go."

"So, Master Levi purchased you, not because he wanted you as a slave, but to get back at your father?"

"He did," Cager said. "Right before he moved on to look at other indentured servants, he leaned over close to my father's ear and said, 'Don't worry. I'll give your lad my undivided attention! Every day for the rest of your life, you'll have to wonder where your son is, and how he's being treated just like I've spent the rest of my life wondering where Roisin is and how you've been treating her. I heard she died on the way over here. Sounds like you've lost her too. Too bad, my friend."

Finney didn't mean to cry, but how could he not? Slave life was anything but fair.

Cager was so wrapped up in telling his story that he didn't even notice the effect it was having on Finney. "Had my father known the spirit planned to split us up or that Master Levi was a part of this, he would never have agreed to come to the new world. And now, after seeing how things go here, I'm worried about my father. With his bum leg, I'm sure he can't do as much work as the other slaves. That means he's not as valuable, and he could easily be killed."

Finney wished he had words of hope to share, but nothing came to mind. Especially not after everything he had witnessed since coming to the colonies, or the new world as Cager called it. More than likely, if Cager's father were still alive, he wouldn't be for long.

Cager stopped talking and for the first time noticed Finney's tears. "Are you crying because of what I've been through or because it's stirring up memories of what you've dealt with?"

"I'm crying for lots of reasons," Finney admitted. "For one, up until recently I've just known Master Levi was my Uncle Keir. He looks and talks just like him. But the longer I'm here, and the more things I hear, the more I realize he can't possibly be my uncle.

"I would have to agree with you," Cager said. "If Master Levi's real name was Keir, my father would have called him that, especially if they knew each other since they were teenagers. It's possible Master Levi and your uncle are related somehow though. There were a lot of big families in Limerick. And you know how much a lot of relatives, even distant ones, look alike."

Finney shook his head. Wiping his eyes he said, "Honestly, I know it's not him. Uncle Keir would never treat people this way. I'm ashamed of myself for even thinking Uncle Keir could possibly stoop so low."

Chapter Thirty-One

News from Afar

That late-night talk with Cager raised Finney's curiosity level. Every slave on that plantation had a story. How did everybody end up there? He knew he would never be able to remember everybody's tales, but he was going to start asking around. And the best place to start would be with the newest arrivals.

Since a woman was working next to him and there were no mulattos close enough to hear, he initiated a conversation. "It sure is a beautiful day out, isn't it?"

"Yes, it is," the lady smiled.

"I'm Finney."

"Nice to meet you, lad. I'm Genevieve."

As the two continued working, Finney asked Genevieve if the Stone plantation was the first one she'd been on.

"No, baby, it's sure not," she said. "I was on another plantation for the past three years. I always prided myself in submitting to my master and mistress, regardless of how cruel they were. But all that changed a while back when they brought in this new slave. I'd have to guess she was somewhere around the age of seven or eight. She had beautiful red hair and bright blue eyes, just like yours. Now that I think of it, she looked just like you, except that she was smaller and had longer hair."

Finney felt his ears perk up. Had Genevieve served on a plantation where his sister was?

The lady continued. "The mistress was harder on that girl than she was on anybody else. I never could understand why. She'd yell at her over every little thing. She'd smack her, push her, hit her with switches. I tried to stay out of it, but I couldn't do it anymore. I'm a mother myself, and my babies were taken from me years ago. But that's another story for another time. I wasn't about to allow some defenseless girl to be abused like that."

Finney could see the pain in Genevieve's eyes. "What happened?"

I became the biggest rebel Master Carlson had ever seen. I started going around to all the other slaves and plotting an uprising. I went out of my way to make both my master my mistress hate me. I'd *accidentally* trip and fall, throwing my water in their faces. I got sick one time and vomited on Master Carlson's head as I walked by him." Genevieve giggled. "He whipped the fire out of me for that one, and I didn't even cry. I hated those people so bad because of how they treated that girl."

"What was the girl's name?" Finney asked.

"Glenna, if I remember correctly."

Finney straightened his back and burst into tears. "Glenna? I have a sister about that age, and Glenna's her name. Was she still alive when you left?"

"Oh, my," Genevieve said. "She most certainly was, child. They sent me off because they didn't want me influencing the other slaves. But Glenna was still there, strong and healthy as could be."

"Where is Master Carlson's plantation?"

"Baby, I couldn't tell you if I wanted to. They wrapped a blindfold around my head on my way to and from that plantation. I have no idea."

"How long do you think it took you to get from the Carlson plantation to the place where Master Levi bought you?"

"I don't know. A couple of hours, maybe?"

"And from that plantation to this one?" Finney asked eagerly.

"I'd guess a couple of more hours. Don't you start thinking about running off to find her now, lad. You know what'll happen to you if you do. And besides, I have no idea what direction they brought me in from."

Finney grinned. "I know what you're saying, ma'am. Thanks for telling me about my sister."

A Note from the Author

Thank you so much for reading *Infuriated*, the second book in my white slave series. As an independently published author, I heavily rely on word-of-mouth advertising in order to get my books in front of as many potential readers as possible. If you enjoyed this book, would you mind telling your social media friends about it? Another way you could help me would be by leaving an honest review on Amazon.

A third book, *Distressed*, will be added to this series as soon as I can get it written as I'm certain you're dying to find out if Finney is able to somehow reunite with his little sister, Glenna. Follow me on Facebook to be notified when the third book comes out!

OTHER BOOKS BY JR THOMPSON

The Worthy Battle Series
Rebuilding Alden
Redirecting Billy
Reprogramming Carlos
Reforming Dawson
Renovating Elliot
Refurbishing Felipe

The Harmony Series
Hidden in Harmony
Fighting for Farmington
Terrors of Troy
Storms at Shelton

**Subscribe to my free newsletter to learn about
current works in progress, and to have an**

opportunity to read my newest book before it's available to the general public.

Follow me on Facebook

Lightning Source UK Ltd.
Milton Keynes UK
UKHW042203150223
417096UK00010B/149

9 781733 767378